"We migh[...] here."

Grant took off his wool shirt and laid it on the cold tile floor. "Care to sit down?"

The inside of a locked safe was a long way from candlelight and roses, but Susan thought his gesture incredibly romantic. "Thank you."

She settled on his shirt, and Grant sat beside her with his arm draped around her shoulders. She snuggled against him, and when she looked up, he kissed her.

He nuzzled her ear. "I wish we knew what Johnny was doing out there. If I knew for sure that he wouldn't come charging in here with his gun cocked, I'd make love to you, Susan."

"Right here? On the cold hard floor?"

"You're not really shocked," he said.

"Not at all." She felt the same way. "We'll get out of this, Grant. We'll have a whole lifetime to make love."

"You've always been an optimist," he said.

She kissed him, slowly, savoring the taste of him. "And you've always been my hero."

Dear Reader,

In the Colorado mountains, snow comes in on a gust of wind, reaching blizzard conditions in a matter of minutes. Here, the Rampart Mountain Rescue Team is never lonely. But this year there's even more activity than usual for the team, as not only Mother Nature but also mystery is swirling in their midst.

Get snowbound with the ROCKY MOUNTAIN RESCUE trilogy by three of your favorite Intrigue authors. For thrills, chills and adventure, ROCKY MOUNTAIN RESCUE is the place to be. In the next two months, look for #454 *Watch Over Me*, by Carly Bishop and #459 *Follow Me Home*, by Leona Karr.

We hope you enjoy all the books in the ROCKY MOUNTAIN RESCUE trilogy, where an icy blizzard rages…and heated passions burn!

Regards,

Debra Matteucci

Debra Matteucci
Senior Editor & Editorial Coordinator
Harlequin Books
300 East 42nd Street
New York, NY 10017

Forget Me Not
Cassie Miles

Harlequin Books

TORONTO • NEW YORK • LONDON
AMSTERDAM • PARIS • SYDNEY • HAMBURG
STOCKHOLM • ATHENS • TOKYO • MILAN
MADRID • WARSAW • BUDAPEST • AUCKLAND

ISBN 0-373-22449-4

FORGET ME NOT

This edition published by arrangement with Harlequin Books S.A.

® and TM are trademarks of the publisher. Trademarks indicated with ® are registered in the United States Patent and Trademark Office, the Canadian Trade Marks Office and in other countries.

Printed in U.S.A.

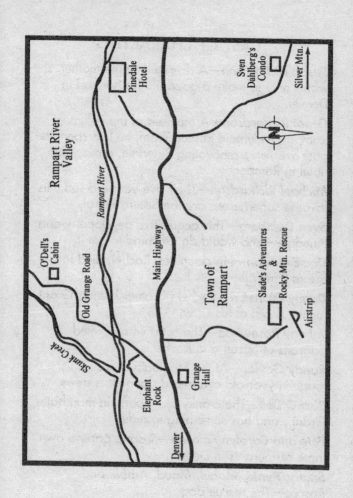

CAST OF CHARACTERS

Susan Richardson—A divorced single mother, she wants only to make a good life for her son in Denver.

Grant Richardson—A member of the volunteer Rampart Mountain Rescue Team, he has spent the past five years renovating Pinedale, a mountain hotel in Rampart.

Michael Richardson—Their five-year-old son. His favorite superheroes are the Saturn Patrol.

Sven Dahlberg—This acquisitive developer wants Pinedale—and would do anything to get it.

Doc Evanston—His daughter, Rachel, died in a fire at Pinedale.

Donny Evanston—Rachel's brother blames Grant for the death of his sister.

Johnny Rosewood—The artist who painted portraits of Susan and Rachel.

Randy Gaylor—At the Mountain Rescue, this fourteen-year-old overheard dangerous news.

Bart O'Dell—The cranky old mountain man hates Grant…and has something to hide.

Pete and Carolyn Falcone—Susan's parents own three restaurants in Denver.

Snuffy, Pyrite, Mabel, Maud, Amble and Roscoe—The rescue dogs.

Chapter One

For years, months and weeks, he'd bided his time. Day after day, from the cadmium glow of dawn until the velvet black of midnight, he'd waited. The need for revenge had built within him, one brick after another in a wall of isolation, a barrier as high as the snow-tipped peaks that rose into the blue Colorado skies.

Now, there were only minutes left.

His partner, Cyrus, sat beside him in the Jeep, fidgeting again. What was wrong with this guy?

"Cyrus? You're not getting cold feet, are you?"

"I'm cold all over," he complained in a voice too small for his large body. "There ain't no heat in this thing."

"We won't be in this piece of junk for long."

Cyrus slumped his shoulders as if the weight of his huge, empty head were too heavy to support. "I been thinking."

"Let me do the thinking."

"We're not going to hurt the kid, are we? Because I like kids, and it don't seem right."

"We won't hurt him." How many times did he

have to explain? "We'll give the kid a sedative. He'll sleep through the whole thing."

"Are you sure?" Cyrus stroked the stubble on his broad chin. "The kid's going to be scared without his mommy."

"Don't worry. I'll take care of Mommy."

She was integral to his plan. To achieve his full measure of vengeance, the Richardson family would be torn apart, they would suffer, as he had suffered. And then Susan would have to die.

"ARE WE THERE YET?"

"Not yet." Susan Richardson glanced in her rear-view mirror. The car behind her was following much too close.

"How many more minutes?"

Her five-year-old son, Michael, studied the face of his Saturn Patrol wristwatch. Such a serious boy! When he was a chubby, laughing, bald-as-a-soccer-ball baby, he was far easier to handle. Recently, he'd begun to ask more difficult questions.

"Mom? What time do we get there?"

"Between one-thirty and two o'clock. Exactly."

He rolled his eyes. "That's not eggs-act!"

"Guess not." But she couldn't estimate the precise minute when they would arrive at the Rampart Mountain Rescue Station, where they would meet her ex-husband, Grant. Although there was very little traffic on the two-lane mountain highway, Susan knew there might be unexpected delays—unforeseen hazards that lay ahead.

For example, the idiot who was tailgating her might smash into the bumper of her brand-new Subaru sedan. Or there might be a rockslide on the road. A sudden snarl of traffic from skiers. Bad weather.

When they'd left Denver early this morning, the radio weathermen had predicted blizzard conditions in the mountains for tomorrow. Today, however, under the January sun, the fields of snow and the glacial peaks on either side of the wide Rampart River Valley shimmered like cold diamonds. Today was a beautiful, blue-sky, Rocky Mountain day.

But the blizzard was coming. Susan could feel its approach. At their last stop for gas, before ascending Rabbit Ears Pass, she'd tasted moisture in the air.

Michael waved the cell phone he'd gotten from her purse. "Can I call Randy, now?"

"Not quite yet, honey. You've got to be real close in the mountains. There's too much interference for the signal to get through."

He stuck the little flip phone into the pocket of his parka and took out his Game Boy. His eyebrows pulled down in concentration, and Susan was struck by his resemblance to his father—the same stubborn jaw, blue eyes, thick chestnut hair and fair skin that sunburned easily.

In many ways, Susan was the opposite. She had her Italian father's jet-black hair, which she wore in a practical wedge cut. Her eyes were hazel and her complexion fair, like her Welsh mother's.

Michael looked up. "Me and Dad are going to have fun. We're going to play with the dogs and go skiing."

"I know." Her own cross-country skis were on the rack atop the car. Susan hoped to get in a little skiing herself before the drive back to Denver tonight.

"How come you don't stay with me and Dad?"

This was one of those difficult questions, and she tried to avoid a complicated answer. "I need to get back to town. Grandpa Pete needs me at the restaurant."

"Do you love me, Mommy?"

"I love you a hundred times a bazillion."

"Do you love Daddy?"

Ouch!

She'd left Grant two years ago, and they'd been divorced for nearly a year, but she still wasn't over him. Did she love him? Though it pained her, Susan had to answer yes to that question. But could they live together? Not a chance. "Your dad and I don't get along very well. The important thing is that we both love you, Michael."

Susan turned left off the main road onto the six-mile stretch that led directly to the Rampart Mountain Rescue Station. This graded, snow-packed road conformed to the winding course of Skunk Creek through fenced land that was owned by one of the high-country ranchers. There were no cabins along this road and stands of ponderosa pine hemmed both sides. Since the terrain was relatively flat, Michael probably could telephone Randy Gaylor.

Before she could tell her son to make his call, she noticed that the Jeep following her had also taken the turnoff. Once again, he was tight behind her. Why was he in such a hurry? At the nearest wide spot in the road, she would pull over and let him go around her.

But it looked like he was ready to make the first move. He was speeding up to pass.

Politely, Susan slowed. She would be delighted to have this creep off her tail.

When he came even with her, she glanced into the filthy, beat-up Jeep. Two men in ski masks sat side by side in the front seat. Though ski masks weren't unusual attire in this part of the country, it was odd that they would wear them inside their car.

The Jeep cut ahead of her—too close! What was he doing? Was he trying to cause an accident?

In an instant of clarity, she knew. For several miles he'd been following her, waiting for this chance, stalking her. Now, there were no other cars in sight. No nearby houses. If she hit the Jeep, she and Michael would be stuck on this desolate road. She felt an edgy stillness at the core of her being, like the last flickering sunlight before a winter blizzard.

Fighting to escape the inevitable disaster, Susan punched the brakes and cranked the steering wheel, swerving. She narrowly avoided the snow and trees at the roadside.

Red taillights flashed in front of her. Frantically, she fought to control the skid, but she couldn't stop.

With a sickening crunch, her front fender plowed into his rear. Instantly, the car's air bags exploded. She was blinded. All the safety warnings about children and air bags flashed through her mind. "Michael! Are you all right?"

He was giggling. Or screaming. She couldn't tell which as she flailed at the deflating bag. "Michael!"

His laughing blue eyes peered over the passenger-side bag. "This is so neat! Wait'll I tell Dad."

She stared toward the Jeep. The two men in ski masks were out of their vehicle, coming toward them. They approached quickly. Something about their attitude told her that she didn't want to talk with these guys.

"Michael, lock your door."

She hit her own lock as the man reached for it. Michael wasn't as fast.

The passenger door swung wide open. A tall man, bulky with ski clothes, clamped a gloved hand around Michael's upper arm.

My God, what was happening? Susan kept her voice low, not wanting to frighten Michael. "Let him go. Let go of my son."

"What's your name, kid?" The gruff voice was muffled beneath the red, patterned ski mask.

"Michael Richardson," he responded.

"Well, Michael Richardson, you tell your mom to do what we say and nobody will get hurt."

"I heard you," Susan said. She pushed the air bag aside and caught hold of Michael's other arm. Her instinct was to attack like a mother bear whose cub was threatened. "We don't want trouble. I'll do whatever you say."

"Unlock your door."

With trembling fingers, she clicked the button.

The second man, in a faceless black ski mask, flung open her door. Roughly, he yanked her out from behind the steering wheel, away from Michael. Grabbing her shoulders, he slammed her against the rear door of her car. A hard blow, but she experienced no pain. Her only thoughts were for her son. She had to protect him. What would happen if she fought back? Her attacker wasn't much taller than her own five feet six inches. Could she overpower him? Could she grab Michael and run?

Then he shoved her hard, and she stumbled forward onto her hands and knees. Her ungloved palms bruised on the frozen surface of the snow-packed road. He pulled back his heavy hiking boot and lashed out with a hard kick to her rib cage.

"Get up!" he ordered.

"Stop it!" Michael shouted. "Don't hurt my mom."

"It's okay, Michael." Wincing, she scrambled to her feet and confronted her assailant. "What do you want?"

His leather-gloved hand caught her by the throat. His ski mask was inches from her face. "This is a kidnapping."

A kidnapping? That was insane! She wasn't an heiress. "Why?"

"Shut up, Susan."

"How do you know my name? Who are you?"

"Shut up and listen." He tightened his grip, choking her. "We want four hundred and fifty thousand dollars. You've got twenty-four hours to get it. Small bills. Unmarked. Understand?"

Her windpipe was crushed. She could hardly breathe, much less speak.

He shouted in her face. "Do you understand me?"

She forced her head to nod.

"Good."

He released her, and Susan bent double, gasping. Her lungs ached with each gulp of ice-cold air. Her injured ribs throbbed painfully.

He reached inside the car and pulled her keys from the ignition. "If you tell anybody, except your ex-husband, the kid's dead. No sheriff. No FBI. No-body."

She heard Michael crying, and the sound of his fear tore at her heart. As the kidnapper went around to the rear of the car, she begged him, "Take me with you.

My son needs me. He's just a little boy. Please take me with you.''

"How the hell are you going to get the money if you're holed up with us? Not very smart, Susan. Here's what we're going to do. You don't tell anybody about this, except your ex. I'll contact you at Pinedale."

Pinedale was the hotel Grant had been renovating for the past three years. When she'd divorced him, she'd sworn never to set foot inside the place again.

"Let me stay with Michael," she pleaded desperately. "If you want ransom from my father, I can call him on the phone. He'll pay."

He drew back his arm and pitched her car keys. They soared through the air and disappeared in the snow-covered pines beyond the road.

The man in the black mask signaled to his partner. "Let's go."

The bigger kidnapper dragged Michael toward their Jeep.

"Mommy!" he wailed. "Mommy, help me!"

"I'm coming!" Driven by unreasoning terror, she started toward him. But her panic made her clumsy. Her boots slipped.

The man in the black ski mask stepped forward to block her way. "Do exactly what I said and the kid won't get hurt."

She lashed out. A wild jab connected with his chest. He staggered. Madly, she took another swing.

He caught her wrist. "Touch me again and I'll break Mikey's little arm."

His voice was colder than the slicing mountain wind. Behind the mask, his brown eyes burned, hard and determined.

Numbly, she recoiled. There was nothing she could do. Michael was already in the Jeep. Her son was being torn from her, and there was nothing she could do to stop it.

"Don't move," he said. "You stand right here like a good girl. Show me you can cooperate, and I won't hurt your boy."

"Whatever you say. I'll get the money. Just don't hurt him. Please. Don't hurt him."

He went to the Jeep, climbed into the driver's side and fired up the engine.

Time stood still for Susan Richardson. Her son, her reason for living, was being stolen from her and abducted into an uncertain future. This sort of nightmare happened to other people, people she read about in the newspapers. Not to her. Not to her son.

The Jeep whipped around in a U-turn and sped past her, heading back to the main highway. Desperate, she raced after them, with her arms outstretched, her fingers straining toward her son. But the Jeep pulled away and left her shivering in bereft agony.

"No!" The single word wrenched from her throat and echoed impotently across the sparkling, snow-covered vista.

GRANT RICHARDSON paced back and forth outside the offices of Slade's Adventures. The premises were designed to look like a rustic mountain lodge, but the interior of the two-story, log-sided structure was as modern as the satellite dish affixed to the roof beside an antique weather vane and a wind sock in the shape of a red-scaled fish. Slade's Adventures, owned by Jack Slade, also served as the operations base for the volunteer Rampart Mountain Rescue team.

The wide plateau, directly in front of Grant, accommodated an unmanned landing strip for small planes and a heliport. Farther down the landing strip was a prefab hangar, big enough for a couple of small planes and Slade's luxury chopper, which he used for search and rescue as well as for ferrying extreme skiers into the backcountry.

Grant stared at his wristwatch, willing the hands to move faster. It was now after two o'clock, and Susan was officially late. Typical! She was always late, always biting off more than she could chew. And when her projects got out of hand, which they invariably did, she would shrug and laugh and start over.

In spite of his impatience, he felt the familiar twinge that came whenever he thought of Susan. The memory of her laughter haunted him. So many times, since their separation and divorce, he'd imagined her gentle voice, lifting in ripples of sheer delight. He would think that he heard her laughter on the main street of Rampart and look up suddenly, expecting to see Susan running toward him, her long black hair flying in the wind and her cheeks rosy with the cold.

Not anymore. Her long hair was cut short. And she seldom smiled when she saw him.

Grant kept the memory of happier times alive in his heart and in the portrait of Susan he'd had done by a local artist, Johnny Rosewood, who had used a photograph that Grant had taken when Susan was pregnant. The painting hung in the lobby at Pinedale. Though he'd tried to keep the portrait in his bedroom, he found that waking up to Susan's laughing hazel eyes disturbed him too much. He didn't need his ex-wife in his bedroom—not that any other woman had taken up residence there.

He should start dating again. Now that his renovations at the turn-of-the-century Pinedale Hotel were
finally complete, he had the time. After the sixty-
room hotel opened next weekend to almost-full book-
ings from two ski clubs, he would have the money to
start a new life.

Right now, however, Grant was close to broke.
He'd spent all of his savings and every penny of the
four-hundred-and-fifty-thousand-dollar insurance pay-
ment he'd received after the fire.

As he watched, a single-engine Cessna glided
across the azure sky like a white-winged seagull. As
the plane positioned itself for a landing, Grant recognized the logo on the tail rudder. The private plane
belonged to Sven Dahlberg, the man who wanted to
develop Rampart and turn it into another Vail. "Not
a seagull," he muttered. "A buzzard, looking for car-
rion."

A teenage boy, Randy Gaylor, came out of Slade's
Adventures to stand beside Grant and watch the landing. Randy was the fourteen-year-old son of Jill Gaylor, the widowed California woman who'd come to
work for Slade's Adventures several months ago, and
who had performed the seemingly impossible task of
getting Jack Slade organized.

"Hey, Grant," Randy said. In spite of the crisp
cold, he wore no hat or gloves. His parka flapped
open around his skinny teenage body that seemed to
run on an inexhaustible supply of energy and heat.
He pointed up at the Cessna. "He's cutting it kind of
short over the trees, isn't he?"

"Consider the pilot," Grant said. "Sven Dahlberg
isn't known for being cautious."

"You don't much like Sven, do you?"

"We're competitors."

Grant frowned but withheld further comment. His ethics kept him from talking bad about the developer who was planning a major condominium complex and ski resort at Silver Mountain. But it wasn't a secret that he and Sven disagreed on practically everything—from the environment to the choice of building materials.

Grant had taken more than five years to meticulously restore the historic Pinedale Hotel to its former glory. His motivation went far beyond profit. He hoped Pinedale would celebrate the atmosphere of the Old West, when prospectors, adventurers and sportsmen still looked to Colorado as a promised land of wonder and beauty. At the same time, he was careful to preserve the present-day landscape, taking the long way around to avoid cutting through a stand of aspen, installing water-saving toilets and carefully hiding solar-heating panels in the hotel gables.

Sven, on the other hand, wanted to bulldoze the hillsides, whip together condos and charge top dollar for the space.

The Cessna touched down in a seamless landing and taxied toward the hangar. Beautiful! Sven might be a jerk, but he knew how to fly a plane.

Again, Grant pushed back his parka cuff and stared at his wristwatch. It was a quarter past two.

Beside him, Randy shifted his weight restlessly from one foot to the other, unable to stand still for more than two minutes at a stretch. "What are you doing this weekend, Grant?"

"Michael's coming to stay with me."

"Cool." With a careless swipe, Randy pushed his longish brown hair off his forehead. "I guess that means my mom shouldn't call you for rescues. Right?"

Grant would never take himself completely off the roster. "Only for extreme emergencies. Or situations where my dogs might be needed."

"Like an avalanche," Randy said knowledgeably.

For a California kid, Randy had caught on quickly when it came to working in the snow. He was helpful when Grant practiced rescue missions with Snuffy and Pyrite, two golden retrievers he'd never managed to train as sled dogs and used as trackers. "You could probably run an avalanche survivor search by yourself," Grant told him.

Randy's skinny chest puffed up beneath his parka. "Yeah?"

"You're good with animals."

"Thanks."

Randy smiled to himself. A compliment from Grant Richardson was beyond cool. Was he really good with animals? If Grant said so, it must be true.

Ever since the first snowfall, they'd been training the dogs. Just last week, they'd built a snow cave and gotten Jack Slade to hide inside while they buried him alive. Then, Grant showed Randy how to work with the dogs while they searched the field and located Jack using their sense of smell.

Most of the time, the golden retrievers were totally crazed, waggling all over the place and wanting to be petted, but they were really, really fast at finding people hidden in the snow. Grant said they were good at rescue because they liked people so much, and it was their instinct to help anybody who was in danger.

"No school today?" Grant asked.

"Half day," Randy replied. He gestured toward the

outskirts of Rampart, visible through the trees. "After I got out, I walked over here to see if I could help Mom. And it's a good thing I did. She was too hassled to even eat lunch."

"How come?"

"Everybody's calling Mountain Rescue. One of the school buses broke down, and the highway going west is shut down until they can move it. I guess the whole sheriff's department is taking kids back into Rampart to wait for their parents."

"The whole sheriff's department, huh? All three vehicles?"

"Not exactly the LAPD," Randy said.

"Well, I'm glad it's nothing serious."

The big, broad-shouldered man clapped him on the shoulder. Randy wouldn't have minded too much if Grant Richardson were his father, but his mom had said Grant was still hung up on his ex-wife.

"So, Grant, did you bring the dogs to meet Michael?"

"Snuffy, Mabel and Maud are in the truck." He jabbed a thumb toward his heavy-duty black Ford truck in the parking lot. "I left Pyrite home. He gets too crazy when he first sees Michael."

"Mind if I go see them?"

"They'd love it, Randy."

The young man headed toward the truck as Sven Dahlberg marched toward Grant.

"Nice landing," Grant said.

"I don't have a problem flying in the mountains. Not even in a blizzard."

How many times had Grant heard bragging like that before a disaster and then a rescue? Only a half-cocked idiot, like big blond Sven, would think that he could conquer the mountains.

His pretty, redheaded secretary came scampering toward them, carrying Sven's attaché case and her own huge, flowered bag. Her leggings fit like a second skin. Her boots had high heels, and her short parka was more for looks than protection against the elements. She fluttered her eyelashes as she greeted him. "Hello, Grant."

"Hi, Melanie."

Sven possessively wrapped his arm around her shoulders. "Are you chilly, sweetheart?"

"Funny thing." She didn't take her eyes off Grant. "It just got a lot warmer."

"Why don't you run inside and say hi to Jill? I'll be right there, okay?"

After a lingering look at Grant, she did as she was told, and Sven turned his attention back to Grant. "I understand you're going to open Pinedale next weekend."

"That's right. I'm fully booked."

"Congratulations. I know we've had our differences, but I'm impressed with your progress."

"Thanks." Grant turned away, hoping the conversation would end there.

"Hold on a minute," Sven said. "I've got a deal for you, Grant. Since I'm going to be the major developer in this area, I wouldn't mind owning Pinedale myself."

"What the hell are you talking about?"

"I want to buy you out." Sven looked as if he were bracing himself, preparing for a fight. "I'll pay top dollar. Name your price."

"Forget it."

"You're a good builder, Grant. But running a hotel is an entirely different kind of pain in the butt. One crisis after another. Toilets overflow. Heating goes out. Stuff gets busted. Other stuff gets swiped. Training your staff is a full-time job, and they're guaranteed to quit just when you need them the most."

"I'll manage."

"You're an outdoors guy. Not an innkeeper. And certainly not a businessman." His smile mocked sincerity. "Take my word for it. You're going to get bored."

"Well, now, I guess you'd know about that. After all, you're the expert on boredom."

Grant squared his shoulders, coolly confronting Sven. They were the same height and build, but Sven's pale blue eyes were shifty as a weasel. He always looked slimy to Grant. Maybe it was the oil Sven used on his thinning blond hair.

The developer bared his sharp teeth in another tight smile. "Why would you think I'm bored?"

"Your work," Grant said. "It's got to be real dull, tacking up one identical condo after another."

"You're wrong about that. I've got all price ranges."

"Big square boxes and little square boxes," Grant said dismissively. "If you're so happy with your condos, why do you want Pinedale?"

"I don't like competition."

"Get used to it," Grant said. "I'm not selling. I'd pack a load of dynamite in the basement and blast Pinedale to kingdom come, before I'd sell it to you."

"Again?" Sven's eyes narrowed to angry slits. "You've already had one fiery disaster at Pinedale. Are you asking for another?"

"Is that a threat?"

"The Pinedale fire isn't a threat, it's a memory. A lot of people around here aren't going to forget that fire, Grant. Or Rachel's death."

Nor would Grant. The accident, three years ago, had been the worst chapter in his life.

"You've got enemies, Grant," Sven concluded. "Some people around here don't want to see you in charge at Pinedale."

"I'm running a hotel, not a popularity contest."

"They haven't forgiven you. Not Rachel's father or her brother. Not all the people who loved her."

Nor had Grant forgiven himself. His guilt simmered into a familiar tension, a heartache too deep to be dispelled with a shrug and a promise. The burns on his hands had healed, but he could never erase the scars.

As Melanie came bouncing out from Slade's Adventures, Sven headed toward her. Over his shoulder, he said, "If you change your mind, you know where to reach me."

If Michael hadn't been coming this weekend, Grant might have argued harder. He might have indulged in the foolhardy pleasure of firing a sharp jab at Sven's pointed jaw. But Grant didn't want to get riled. And he refused to succumb to the dark mood that descended whenever he remembered the fire.

This weekend he would spend time with his son. Whether they were outdoors or settled in with popcorn and those Saturn Patrol videos that Michael loved, this was going to be quality time, a good time for bonding and getting to know each other.

As Sven's Land Rover pulled away from the parking lot, with the perky redhead waving from the pas-

senger-side window, Grant saw another figure on the
road. A woman on cross-country skis was coming in
his direction, pumping hard with her arms and legs
on the uphill approach. Even though she was wearing
a new parka, he immediately recognized his ex-wife.

Why was she on skis? Where the hell was Michael?
He ran down to meet her. "Susan?"

She was breathing hard. Her flushed cheeks were
marked with the tracks of her tears.

"Susan, what's wrong?"

She drove her ski poles into the snow at the side
of the road with a violent force. Her beautiful face
contorted with strong, unreadable emotion. Gasping,
she said, "They took Michael."

Chapter Two

Susan had to make him understand. She had to explain to Grant—a man of action—why he couldn't charge off, organize a search party and track down the kidnappers like the beasts they were. In her mind, she replayed the kidnapper's cold threat. *"I'll break Mikey's little arm."* His cruelty was as real as the bruises on her body, and she was convinced that her son's survival depended on doing exactly as the kidnappers had ordered.

"Susan, what the hell is going on?"

She sought understanding in Grant's blue eyes. Instead, she saw anger and disgust.

"Damn it, Susan. Where's Michael?" He tugged at her arm and she winced at the resulting pain in her ribs where the kidnapper had kicked her.

Immediately, Grant released her. No doubt he'd misinterpreted her reflex as another example of her supposed hatred for him—as if she couldn't stand to be touched by his hands. It wasn't true. At this most desperate moment, more than anything, she longed for the closeness they once had shared.

She needed for him to be gentle, patient and strong.

As never before, they needed to act as partners. She and Grant must work together to save Michael.

"We have to do as they say, Grant. Otherwise, they'll hurt Michael."

"Who?" he demanded. His stubborn jaw lifted.

"You've got to listen to me." Desperation sharpened the tone of her voice. "Just this once. We have to do things my way. Promise me."

"Fine. Whatever." He threw up his hands in exasperation. "Tell me what happened. Start at the beginning."

"I was on the turnoff from the main road, the back route that comes directly here instead of going through Rampart. I was in the trees. A Jeep cut me off. I couldn't stop, and I ran into the back of him. The air bags exploded. Two men came out of the Jeep." Choked by emotion, she whispered, "They took Michael."

"Why?"

"Kidnapping. They kidnapped our son."

She heard the sharp intake of his breath. Whatever Grant had been expecting, this wasn't it. His eyes slowly closed as he digested the horror of what she'd said. He winced. The color drained from his face. When his eyelids lifted, his blue eyes reflected her own devastation and helplessness.

"Why?" he asked. "We're not rich. Your father has money, but he's not a millionaire. Or is he?"

Actually, he was. For the past twenty years, Pete Falcone had operated successful restaurants in Denver. Including home and assets, he was a millionaire three times over. But his fortune wasn't liquid. It would be difficult for him to come up with four hundred and fifty thousand dollars in cash. "My father is very well-off."

"Do you think the kidnappers are after your father's money?"

No. Her intuition told her that the man who had spoken to her wasn't driven by the desire for money. There was something else he wanted. Satisfaction. Vengeance?

Susan frowned and shook her head. She didn't know for sure. Confusion reigned in her mind. "I can't answer that, Grant."

Her lips pressed tightly together, holding back the cries that had been building within her since the moment Michael had been torn from her.

Grant held out his arms, offering solace.

Did she dare to accept his gesture of comfort? It had taken all of her willpower to resist the magnetism between them.

"Come on," he said.

Fearfully, Susan stepped into his embrace. Pressed against her, the contours of his muscular body were shockingly familiar. So many nights she'd yearned for Grant's soothing caress. She'd missed his physical presence so very much.

Her arms tightened around him. Closer, she needed to be closer, to be a part of him, to feel his strength. Her ribs and bruises ached, but her physical pain was nothing compared to her need.

Clinging to each other, breathing as one, they met at a profound level. Michael was their child, and he was in danger. Nothing else was important. Nothing else in the world existed for them. She and Grant were helpless victims in a barren void where there was no sky, no earth, no air. Their only reality was an all-consuming concern for their son.

Grant stepped away from her. He cleared his throat, and she recognized the dispassionate air of authority he always assumed when working on mountain rescues. "Did you recognize the men?"

"No. They wore ski masks."

"Their voices?"

It would be so easy to let him take charge. Grant was a natural leader, and she was tempted to step back and allow him to handle this dangerous situation. What did she know of danger? Susan had never claimed to be a brave woman.

"Susan? Did you notice anything about their voices?"

"I heard both of them speak. I didn't know them."

"Describe the men," he said.

She couldn't do things his way. Grant would round up a posse and go after the kidnappers. She wouldn't take that risk with Michael's life. "Don't do this," she warned.

"I'm only trying to understand."

"It doesn't matter what they look like," she said. "We're supposed to go to Pinedale and wait for their call. All I want to do is pay the ransom and get my son back."

He persisted, "They both wore parkas, didn't they? What color were the parkas? Please, Susan. Help me out, here."

She couldn't refuse this basic information. He deserved to know as much as she did.

Speaking quickly, she said, "Their jackets were navy blue and gray. The man who did most of the talking wasn't very tall, probably only five feet eight inches. He had brown eyes. The other one was bigger, husky, strong."

She flashed on the mental picture of the larger man in the red ski mask carrying Michael. Her son had been struggling, but the kidnapper held him easily.

"Do you think they're locals?" Grant asked.

She shook her head, unwilling to speculate.

Grant continued, "They have to be somebody who's familiar with this territory. Otherwise, they wouldn't know which road you'd turn on."

"They followed me for a long time, waiting for the right chance."

"What about the Jeep? Did you recognize the Jeep?"

"It was old, beat-up and so filthy that I couldn't read the license plate." Firmly, she said, "We're not going after them."

"If you can describe their vehicle," he said, "we can alert the sheriff's office without telling them why we're looking for the Jeep."

"They specifically said not to contact the sheriff. Besides, there was nothing special about this Jeep. It reminded me of those little old junkers that so many people around here keep for snowplowing in winter."

"But you hit the rear end," he said.

"One of the taillights is out." She felt like he was sucking her in. Against her better judgment, he was convincing her. "We should go to Pinedale now, Grant. To wait for the phone call."

"How long ago did this happen?"

"Michael was counting the minutes until he got here." *Are we there yet? Are we there?* His small voice echoed through her mind.

"Susan, what time?"

"We took the turnoff at one-forty."

Grant checked his watch. "It's two twenty-five. Almost an hour. Damn."

"What?"

"Susan, why didn't you drive here?"

"The kidnapper took my car keys and threw them in the snow beyond the road. I thought of going to the main road and trying to flag somebody down. But I had my skis on top of the car, and I thought it would be faster if—"

"You don't have a spare key?"

"No."

Disgusted, he said, "I always told you to keep a spare under the hood in case you lock yourself out."

He'd told her a lot of things. "It's a new car. I haven't had time to make extra keys."

"How did they get to you? Why didn't you have the doors locked?"

"I didn't think of that until it was too late. Everything happened so fast."

"Brilliant!" He spat the word at her. "You're so damned careless, Susan."

"What are you saying? That this is my fault?"

"If I'd been with you, Michael never would have been kidnapped."

"How can you say that?"

"Because it's true." He straightened his posture. The midafternoon sunlight burnished the broad shoulders of his parka. "If I'd been with you, I could have stopped them."

His piercing blue eyes sliced at the last tenuous thread of her self-control. His cruel accusation shot straight to the target. Bull's-eye! She hadn't been strong enough to stop the kidnappers. She hadn't been smart enough to lock the car doors, hadn't thought ahead to hide an extra key.

Like it or not, Susan was a single mother, prey to dangers that wouldn't happen if she had a big strong man to protect her and Michael. Vulnerability came with the territory of being divorced.

But it wasn't the first time she'd made a mistake. And right now, she couldn't indulge in self-recrimination. She had to think of Michael and convince her ex-husband not to go after the kidnappers. They had to be smart.

Grant turned on his heel and stormed up the snow-packed road. From the parking lot, she heard the welcoming yips of his dogs.

"Grant! Where are you going?" Frantically, she grabbed her ski poles and started after him. Her voice cracked as she shouted again, "Wait! Grant, wait for me!"

Beside his truck, he pivoted and faced her. "I'm taking over."

"The hell you are." She glided up beside him.

Three cheerful dog faces peeked out from the truck bed. Mabel and Maud—two malamutes—and Snuffy, a golden retriever. They were panting and excited.

"Be still," Grant ordered his dogs.

Though they didn't retreat, the three animals took on a more serious demeanor. Their wagging enthusiasm was subdued. The well-trained canines were alert, waiting for the next command.

"The road to the west of town is blocked," Grant said. "One of the school buses stalled. If the Jeep went that way, I might be able to catch them."

"Don't try anything. They said not to try to follow them."

"I don't take orders from kidnappers."

"This isn't about you." She unfastened her bindings and kicked off the skis. "It's about Michael. The kidnappers will hurt him if we don't do what they say."

Grant hesitated as a moment of doubt tempered his need for aggressive action.

Susan continued in a rush. "They told me I couldn't contact the police or the FBI or anybody but you. Believe me, Grant. When I tried to fight one of them, he looked me in the eye and said if I touched him again, he'd break Michael's arm. Do you hear me?"

"Yes."

He was terse, angry, unreasonable. This was the Grant she'd divorced, the insensitive Grant. When she'd left him, she'd turned away from this Grant, the man who refused to communicate. When she'd dragged him into marriage counseling, he'd turned rugged silence into an art form. Unfortunately, she didn't have the option of leaving him at this moment.

She had to fight. For Michael's sake.

Matching his determination, she said, "We're supposed to go to Pinedale and wait for their call. And we're going to do what they tell us."

Fury radiated from him in waves. His jaw clenched. The sinews in his neck corded, tight as braided steel. And his eyes—his beautiful eyes that could glow with gentle warmth—took on a silvery glitter. It was a look she'd only seen once before.

In a steady voice, she recalled that moment. "This isn't like the fire, Grant."

It had taken three men to hold him back when he'd realized Rachel was trapped inside the flames. Even then, he'd broken away. His hands and forearms sustained second-degree burns when he'd tried to reach her.

Susan knew that he'd always blamed himself. Somehow, in spite of a vicious conflagration that had consumed the entire kitchen of Pinedale and had melted tin and chrome, Grant had thought he could race inside and rescue Rachel the way he'd rescued so many other people from mountain disasters.

The fire had changed everything. Before the accident, when they'd worked on Pinedale with their partners, Charley and Rachel Beacham, the renovation had been exciting and fun. They'd been full of dreams about the future.

After the fire, Charley had given up his share of Pinedale. He'd left the mountains, wanting nothing more to do with the place where his wife had died. And Grant had become obsessed with the renovations at the hotel. Night and day, he'd worked alone, barely speaking to Susan. He'd ignored their toddler son, Michael. Consumed by his work and exhausted, Grant had stopped talking about anything. He became a different man—angry and sullen.

And their love had chilled. They became adept at sniping, skilled at delivering hurtful barbs.

"You wouldn't let me save Rachel," he said.

"It wasn't just me, Grant. I wasn't the only one who held you back."

"I won't make that mistake with Michael."

"This is different. We're dealing with men, human beings, not a fire that raged out of our control. We can do something about the kidnapping. We will do something."

"What?"

"We're going to be smart. Use our heads. We have to outthink them." He seemed to be paying attention. "First, we'll make it seem as if we're doing what they tell us to do. We'll go to Pinedale."

With a nod, he acknowledged her words. "Do you think they're watching us?"

"I don't know. There were only two of them."

"But they could be working for someone else." He yanked open the passenger door. "Get in the truck."

She eyed him suspiciously, unable to believe that he'd conceded so easily. Though her ex-husband was an intelligent man, who'd enjoyed a successful career as an attorney before settling in Rampart, he was accustomed to solving problems with his physical prowess. Rescue missions. Avalanche searches. Traversing difficult terrain with his dogsled.

"Grant, you have to promise you won't try anything. Promise that we'll go directly to Pinedale."

"I'll do whatever it takes."

As she climbed up into the truck, he slammed the door and turned toward the offices of Slade's Adventures.

She cranked down the window and called to him, "Where are you going?"

"I need to tell Jill Gaylor that I'll be at Pinedale in case anything comes through for me."

"You can't tell her about—"

"I understand." He returned to stand close beside the truck. "I wouldn't tell Jill because there's nothing she can do and she's got her hands full. And you can be damned sure I won't tell Sheriff Perkins. That old fool can barely manage to write parking tickets. I sure as hell wouldn't trust him with my son's safety."

Grant turned away from his ex-wife and his truck and his dogs. He strode toward the rustic-looking lodge behind the landing strip. Though it was only midafternoon, the shadows had begun to lengthen and the trees stood out in sharp relief against the snow-covered hillsides.

The pristine beauty of the endless blue sky mocked him. His son had been kidnapped. The world should reflect the horror that constricted around his heart like a deadly serpent. Without Michael, the heavens should be dismal. The sun should not dare to shine.

Who would have taken his son? Why? Sven Dahlberg wanted Grant to sell the hotel and move away from Rampart, but it was hard to believe that the developer would undertake such a vicious stunt. Kidnapping was a felony. Despite his arrogance, Sven wasn't stupid enough to risk federal charges.

Then who? Even if Pete Falcone was a millionaire, Susan's father didn't seem a likely target for ransom. There were a lot of rich men and women in Denver. And why would kidnappers follow Susan all the way up here to make the grab?

Who? Moments ago, Sven had pointed out that Grant had enemies in town. When Rachel Evanston Beacham had died in the fire, a lot of people had blamed him. They hated him. Enough to hurt Michael? An innocent child?

When he caught these kidnappers, his revenge would be severe. If they were lucky, they would spend the rest of their natural lives in prison.

Inside Slade's Adventures, Grant had an idea where he might find some answers. He closed the door behind him and entered the main office. With its panoramic view, this was a good location to scan the area. To the east, there were forests and trees. To the west, he saw the quiet little town of Rampart. Was Michael in the town? Hidden in a back room? Locked away in a dark closet? A sharp pain twisted in his gut when he thought of his son suffering and afraid.

Jill Gaylor was on the phone, reassuring a mother whose child had not yet returned from school.

"You can pick up your daughter at the sheriff's station," Jill said patiently. She looked up at Grant and winked before continuing, "No, there wasn't an accident. All the children are safe. The bus broke down."

As she continued her conversation, he checked the stack of notes recording other calls. Since many people in the area called on the Mountain Rescue telephone whenever they had a problem, Jill had developed a color-coding system for messages. Her calls from clients and travel agents to Slade's Adventures were completely separate, on white sheets of paper with spaces for detailed information. But there were other colored notes, neatly filed at her desk.

On little While You Were Out notes, in blue, there were calls from people who couldn't reach the only doctor in town and didn't like leaving messages on his machine. Traffic accidents and other minor problems that should go to the sheriff's office were on yellow. Actual emergencies, requiring an alert to the volunteer Rampart Mountain Rescue, were written on hot pink.

Right now there were only two hot-pink notes. One indicated a rescue in progress, airlifting a man who had been stricken with a heart attack in his secluded cabin. Flight for Life helicopters from a Denver hospital had already been dispatched. The other Mountain Rescue note was a warning from the U.S. Forest Service. Avalanche danger was high for today and tomorrow.

While Jill spoke gently into the telephone, calming the nervous parent on the other end, Grant took the opportunity to study the messages for Doc Evanston. If anyone had reason to despise Grant, it was the local GP. His daughter, Rachel, had died in the flames. Grant would never forget the pain etched deeply into Doc's face at the funeral. He'd aged ten years in a few days. His wiry shoulders bowed and he'd leaned heavily on the arm of his son. The doctor's capable hands—the hands that had assisted at Michael's birth—had shivered uncontrollably on that warm August day.

In his heart, Grant knew that Doc hadn't forgiven him. Though they'd avoided outright hostility, the two men hadn't spoken except when necessary on rescues.

Grant found nothing unusual in the two or three messages for Doc Evanston. Jill had merely noted the time and the name of the caller. Apparently the doctor had been out since early this morning.

Grant thumbed through the stack of phone calls from worried parents that should have gone to the understaffed offices of Sheriff Walt Perkins. Mixed among the yellow notes were minor traffic accidents. One caught his eye. Adrian Walker on the Old Grange Road reported that a Jeep had slid off the road near her house. A Jeep? Grant folded the note and stuck it in his pocket.

Jill got off the phone and adjusted the long braid that hung down her back. "There were twenty-seven kids on that bus, and I've heard from almost every one of their parents. You'd think the school bus was never late before."

"People are extra cautious," Grant said, "where their children are concerned."

"Everybody's edgy. Especially since the big blizzard is supposed to hit tomorrow." Glancing out the window, she shrugged. "With the gorgeous weather we're having today, it seems impossible that we might get over thirty inches of new snow tomorrow."

"Colorado weather. If you don't like it, wait five minutes and it'll change."

"What can I do for you, Grant?"

Could he tell her? Would it help? Feigning casualness, he gestured toward the couple of messages for Doc Evanston. "Is Doc out of town?"

"He went skiing today at Silver Mountain. Left me a message this morning that he wouldn't be back at his office until late." She frowned up at Grant. "Do you need to see him?"

"No, I was just curious."

Her business phone rang, and she picked up. "Slade's Adventures, please hold."

Expectantly, she looked up at Grant.

"My son is visiting this weekend," he said. "If you need me, I'll be at Pinedale."

"Got it." She jotted on an aquamarine note and slipped it in a slot marked: Rescue Personnel.

Should he say more? Grant shook his head. "That's all."

"Have fun with Michael."

He averted his face before she noticed the stricken expression he could not hide. The thought that he might never have fun with Michael again hit him hard.

As the black truck with the dogs in the back pulled out of the parking lot, Randy Gaylor stepped out from behind the rock where he'd been hiding. A kidnapping?

When he'd seen Grant and his ex-wife charging at the truck, arguing with each other, he'd made himself scarce. He hadn't wanted to overhear what was going on between them.

But he couldn't help it.

Michael had been kidnapped. That was so freakin' bad, Randy couldn't believe it. The poor little kid!

And Grant couldn't tell anybody. Or else the kidnappers would hurt his son.

Randy was the only person, except for Grant and his ex-wife and the kidnappers, who knew.

He sat down in the snow and wrapped his arms around his knees. What was he going to do? Should he tell his mom? Or Jack Slade? Maybe he should tell Jack.

Or maybe he'd better keep his big mouth shut.

He stared through the sheltering wall of trees at the Mountain Rescue headquarters. There had to be something he could do. Anything. But what?

"Oh, damn."

As Grant drove his truck slowly along Branch Street toward the only stoplight in Rampart, Susan tried to put her fears for Michael on hold. She had to stop thinking about the kidnapping or she would go crazy. Had they hurt her son? What were those men doing to him? He was only five years old, only a baby. He must be terrified, traumatized.

Grant bounced over a pothole and she gasped at the pain emanating from her rib cage.

At least she'd finally convinced her stubborn ex-husband not to launch a rescue that would endanger their son. She adjusted her position on the front seat of his truck. There was nothing else they could do. The best thing was to go to Pinedale and wait for the kidnappers' call.

Looking through the windshield, she noticed changes in the quaint mountain town. Usually, she avoided Rampart when she dropped Michael off. There were too many memories here.

She glanced toward the Victorian-style boarding-house where she and Grant had stayed when they came here for the first time. The three-story, ginger-bread-trimmed house was a charming place that, un-fortunately, sacrificed comfort for antique authentic-ity.

Almost smiling, Susan recalled how the ancient springs on the bed in their second-floor room had creaked in discordant symphony. She and Grant had stifled their giggles like a couple of naughty teen-agers. At that point, they'd been married for almost two years, so there was no longer that urgent need to make love every time they were alone. But that night the passionate light in his breathtaking blue eyes would not be denied. Not that Susan had any desire to refuse him. She'd loved him deeply, and there was nothing more enticing to a woman than a man who adored her. Not wanting to awaken the other guests, they'd moved the comforter to the floor. It was there, according to Susan's best calculations, that Michael had been conceived.

On the following day, she'd fallen in love with the cozy town, the spectacular views, and Pinedale. Though Rampart was too far off the beaten path to attract many tourists, she'd thought it was a good investment because they were buying into a life-style. When they'd purchased the hotel and moved in, she'd found security in the small-town atmosphere. She knew all her neighbors, greeted most of the people she met by their first name. Other than the occasional skiers from Silver Mountain, there weren't many visitors to Rampart.

Now the streets were populated by strangers in ski gear. In the display window of Handy Mercantile, a woman changed the clothing on a mannequin. A sign in the window of the real-estate office advertised time-share condominiums. The previously vacant space next door was occupied by a bakery. The Rampart Ram Tavern was crowded.

"You were right," she said to Grant. "You always predicted that, within five years, Rampart would be as busy as Breckenridge."

"Which is why Pinedale Hotel is going to be a big success," he concluded.

She sighed. "I miss the way it was."

"So do I."

Curiously, she studied his rugged profile. "You do? I thought you wanted change and development."

"Not the way Sven Dahlberg does it. He erects cheap condos to attract people to the area, then sells at inflated prices. The old-timers are either moving out or looking to make a quick buck off the tourists." His eyebrows pulled down in a handsomely craggy scowl. "Maybe he's right. Maybe I should sell Pinedale to him and move on."

She couldn't believe her ears. "You'd sell Pinedale?"

He stopped for the red light. "When you and Mi-

chael were here with me, it was a home. Now, it's...
I don't know. It's too quiet."

Quiet? After the fire he'd criticized her for talking
too much and laughing too loud and humming to herself. "Are you saying that you miss the way I used
to chatter on and on?"

"More than you'll ever know."

Never before had Grant admitted to any regrets,
and she would have pursued this surprising change of
heart if he hadn't turned right at the light.

Immediately, Susan was alert. "Where are you
headed, Grant? This isn't the route to Pinedale."

"I wanted to make a stop at Doc Evanston's
house."

"Why?"

"I'll be quick," he promised.

Grant wanted to investigate the suspicious coincidence. Why had the good doctor chosen this particular day to go skiing? This day, when Michael had
been abducted.

Though Grant didn't want to believe that Doc Evanston had hired the two kidnappers, he might as well
check out the possibility. Since they had to go through
town anyway, it would only take a moment to stop
by and make sure Doc hadn't arranged some kind of
revenge for Rachel's death.

Susan's voice sounded strained. "You didn't answer my question. Why do you want to see Doc Evanston?"

If the doctor had returned from his ski trip and was
relaxing, Grant could dismiss him from the list of
possible kidnappers. On the other hand, if the doctor
had lied about going skiing, his behavior might be
construed as suspicious.

And then what? Questions. Deductions. Logic. Though Grant had spent the past five years working on the reconstruction of Pinedale, his training in law would be valuable.

Vaguely, he avoided telling Susan the exact truth. "Doc isn't in the office today. I wanted to make sure nothing was wrong."

"I don't believe you," she said. "Right now, there's only one thing on your mind. It's the same thing I'm thinking about. The kidnapping."

"Maybe."

"Oh, Grant. Surely you don't suspect Doc Evanston of being involved?"

"It's possible. Rachel's death affected him. Maybe he's decided it's time to get even."

Grant parked in the shoveled driveway beside the tidy, slate-blue house with white trim, where Doc had his practice on the first floor and made his home on the second. The house was on the shady side of the street and, even now at midafternoon, there were shadows. Through an upstairs window, Grant saw the glow of a lamp. Was Doc up there? Was Michael? "I'll be right back. Stay here, Susan."

"Don't tell me to stay. I'm not one of your dogs." She followed him to the front porch. "You promised we'd go directly to Pinedale."

"Actually I didn't give my word. I said I'd do what was necessary." He pressed the doorbell and waited, while Susan stood beside him, fuming.

After a moment, he rang again.

"Nobody's here," Susan said. "Let's go."

Either Doc was still on the ski slopes or he'd gone somewhere else. To check on the kidnappers? Grant reached out and twisted the doorknob. Unlocked, it turned easily in his hand. He stepped inside.

Susan whispered, "What are you doing? You can't just walk in here."

"It seems that I can." He glanced down at her. "If this makes you nervous, wait in the truck."

The front parlor was a waiting room with white tile floors, functional chairs and dog-eared *National Geographic* magazines. On the wall opposite the front door was a display of skiing medals and trophies—the prizes Rachel had won for her outstanding athletic ability. Grant looked away quickly, unwilling to face this memorial to the woman who had died at Pinedale.

Trying to relax, he inhaled deeply. The house was silent, the air touched with a faint medicinal smell.

Through a swing door, there were two small examination rooms, a supply closet and a bathroom. The area was scrupulously clean.

He pushed open the oak door to Doc Evanston's office. A bright halogen lamp shone down on the surface of a heavy, old-fashioned desk. The man sitting behind the desk jumped to his feet when they entered.

His shoulder-length hair was the same bright auburn as Rachel's. His features were eerily similar to hers.

"Grant Richardson," he said. "You bastard."

"You're Donny." If Grant remembered correctly, Rachel's brother lived in the Pacific Northwest. "From Portland?"

"That's right. What the hell are you doing here?"

"I was looking for your father." Or for you, Grant thought. Donny also had a motive for revenge.

"He's not here. That's why I didn't answer the doorbell." Donny came around the desk. His voice was bitter. "I didn't want to be bothered by Dad's patients—all the old biddies with sniffles and the anxious mommies whose babies have stubbed toes. I don't need those headaches."

Apparently, Donny didn't share his father's empathy for the sick and wounded. Grant asked, "Why are you in town?"

"None of your business." He stared at Susan. "You're his wife, aren't you? Or ex-wife? I heard you'd divorced this bum."

With a stiff-legged gait, Susan walked past him. She went to the wall behind the desk and stood, mesmerized, staring up at a large oil painting of Rachel.

Grant recognized the style of Johnny Rosewood, the same artist who had done the portrait of Susan and signed it in the lower right-hand corner with a rose. The energy in the painting was remarkable. With vivid strokes, the artist had captured the fiery sheen of Rachel's hair and the vivacious curve of her lips. She looked so alive. Had this portrait been done before or after her death? It must have been after. Grant couldn't recall meeting Rosewood until after Susan had left him.

Susan reached toward the painting as if she could somehow make contact with her friend. "I miss her."

"Spare me," Donny sneered. "She was my sister. My sweet baby sister. Not a day goes by when I don't think about her."

Susan whirled to face him. Her cheeks flushed a delicate pink, but her eyes were hard and determined as she confronted him. "Where's Michael?"

Chapter Three

Donny's expression of confusion was either well-rehearsed or genuine. Grant couldn't tell which.

"What are you talking about?" Donny barked at Susan. "Who the hell is Michael?"

She spoke slowly as if choosing her words with care. "There's nothing in the world more terrible than losing a family member. A sister. A daughter. Or a son."

"I know. Why are you telling me?"

Grant studied the wiry young man's body language. He was tall but skinny. His shoulders were narrow. Shifting his weight back and forth from one foot to the other, Donny seemed nervous, unduly tense.

"Donny," Grant said, "you know why we're here."

"I don't know what the hell you're talking about, man. But I don't like you being in this house. You don't belong here. After Mom died, this is where we grew up, me and Rachel. This is our house."

"I'm sorry," Susan said. "You must have so many memories."

"I don't want your pity." His voice was a slightly nasal whine. "Not yours. And definitely not his."

He sounded petulant, Grant thought, and imma-ture—though he must have been pushing thirty. Donny appeared to be bitter enough to strike out at Grant by kidnapping Michael. But was he clever enough?

Grant asked, "What are you doing in Rampart, Donny?"

"None of your business! I'm not talking to you." He charged at Grant and shoved him in the chest. "Get out!"

Adrenaline surged in Grant's veins, but he held back. He had no reason to hate Rachel's brother. It was the opposite, in fact. Donny had every motivation to despise him.

"You heard me!" Donny shouted. "Get out!"

"I want answers," Grant said. He watched Donny's face for any sign of deception—shifting eyes, a twitch, licking his lips. "What do you know about Michael?"

"Michael who?"

Susan rushed forward, positioning herself between the two men. "We shouldn't say anything more, Grant. Please."

"You heard the lady," Donny said. "Leave us alone."

"Us?" Was he referring to himself and the kid-nappers?

"Me and my dad." Donny reached past Susan to take another jab at Grant, hitting his shoulder. "Haven't you done enough to hurt this family? You killed my sister."

Grant was staggered by the viciousness of his words, not by the light blow, which was easily de-flected. "Calm down, Donny."

"It's true." Again, Donny reached around Susan to slap at Grant. "My sister died because of that damned hotel, and you were in charge. You should have saved her."

Three years of guilt constricted around Grant, paralyzing him. There was nothing he could offer that would atone for Rachel's death. His conscience wouldn't let go. He'd been through counseling with Susan. On his own, he'd visited a psychologist, who'd told him that he must release the past.

But he couldn't do it. His only escape was to keep himself so busy that he couldn't think, couldn't remember, couldn't relive the fire every night in his dreams.

With pain-filled eyes, he stared at Donny. His resemblance to Rachel was uncanny. Her portrait, her medals, this home where she'd grown up had gouged open his memories.

"Get out!" Donny yelled.

"You want to hit me? Go ahead. I won't fight back."

"Stop it!" Susan shouted at him.

Puzzled, Grant looked down at her. She should have been pleased. He was getting what he deserved, taking his punishment.

Sharply, she said, "Have you forgotten why we're here?"

Michael. Grant shook his head. His shame over Rachel's death had momentarily overshadowed his concern for Michael. How could that be? Rachel was dead. He couldn't help her now. How could he have forgotten that Michael, his only son, was in danger?

Susan was directing him toward the door, offering an apology to Donny, "We're sorry for bothering you. Would you please ask your father to call me at Pinedale when he gets in?''

"I'm not your secretary."

"Fine," she said. "I'll contact him."

They were outside again, and she pushed Grant toward the truck. "I can't believe you. When are you going to quit wallowing in the past?"

"Sometimes I think I'm crazy. If I were a drinking man, I'd be an alcoholic."

"But you're a working man," she said. "A workaholic."

"I've spent a lot of time feeling sorry about Rachel."

"Feeling sorry for yourself." There was no mistaking her outraged fury. "You've always been the big hero, the rescuer who goes out to save people trapped on cliffs, kids who are lost in the forests, avalanche victims. But you failed Rachel, and you can't accept that."

Startled by her accusation, he stopped dead in his tracks. "It's not like you to say that."

"I happen to be a little bit stressed." She stamped her foot in the snow. "Listen to me, Grant. You can't always be the hero. So, at least try not to be a total ass. Get over it."

Amazing! Susan was usually the soul of tact and sensitivity. She didn't make accusations; she made allowances, always trying to understand the other person. She was a peacemaker, who had done everything in her power to heal their marriage.

"Get in the truck," she ordered. "And give me the keys. I'm driving, and we're going to Pinedale."

He held the keys. "I'm driving."

Grant circled to the driver's side. Susan was right

to call him an ass. He'd needed that jolt back to reality. The past was gone. Right now, he needed to figure out how they would rescue Michael.

Backtracking, he drove along the road that led to Slade's Adventures.

"Damn it, Grant. Why are we going this way?"

"Tell me what you think, Susan. Was Donny involved in the kidnapping?"

She hesitated before replying. "He wasn't one of the two men who stopped me."

"He could be working with them," Grant said. "He could have hired them."

When she turned her head toward him, she winced slightly. The strain was beginning to show on her face. The faint shadows around her eyes were as dark as bruises. "Where are we going?"

"Why is Donny in Rampart right now? And where's Doc? These coincidences need explanations."

"Please, Grant," she said with heavy exasperation. "Let's do this my way."

"Give me one hour to investigate. You made good time on your cross-country skis, and I'm sure the kidnappers didn't figure on that. They probably assumed you walked the six miles."

"So?"

"They won't expect you to be at Pinedale for at least an hour."

"That makes sense," she conceded.

"In an hour, I can follow up on a couple of leads. If we can figure out who took Michael and why, we have an advantage. You can see that, can't you?"

"All I know is that as soon as we pay the ransom,

we get Michael back. Nothing else is really important.''

He didn't want to tell her the brutal statistics he'd learned many years ago when he'd worked for the Denver District Attorney's office. Only about thirty percent of reported abductions had a happy ending with the children returned unharmed. ''Come on, Susan. If you won't let me contact the authorities, at least give me this.''

''All right. One hour.''

Retracing her route on the side road from the highway to Slade's Adventures, Grant soon came upon her disabled Subaru sedan. He pulled over, parked on the shoulder and glared at the compact car. The citified vehicle reminded him that she and Michael didn't live in the mountains anymore. God, it was hard to be with her—wanting her and being angry at the same time.

''Well, Susan. You finally got the cute little car you always wanted.''

''It's practical,'' she said. ''And the front-wheel drive handles very well in the mountains.''

''Glad you like it. Of course, if you'd been driving the old van, the kidnappers might have thought twice before they forced you off the road.''

Before she could inform him that a minivan was hardly an unstoppable tank, he was out of the truck. Why wouldn't he ever listen to her? The boxy van was harder to handle than the Subaru sedan—not to mention that it was difficult to park in the city, got poor gas mileage and needed a massive overhaul.

Susan didn't want to waste her breath on their usual sniping exchange. They needed to stay focused, to stay united. For Michael's sake.

She joined Grant at her car, where he stared into the back seat. "Where's Michael's suitcase?"

"It was back there. I didn't notice, but the kidnappers must have taken it with them."

"Damn."

"Why does that bother you? I'd think it was a positive sign that they took Michael's things with him. You know, to make him comfortable."

"I was hoping to find something with Michael's scent."

"His scent?"

"I could give it to Snuffy. She might be able to track the kidnappers."

She bit back the hostile retort that was poised on the tip of her tongue. Though she loved the dogs, and they really were incredible at finding people who were buried in the snow, they weren't bloodhounds.

"What about this?" On the front seat, he found a blue knit cap with a multicolored tassel. "This is Michael's, isn't it?"

She was tempted to say no and avoid the ridiculous charade of having Snuffy dash through the forest trying to please them. "It's Michael's."

"Let's try this. It can't hurt."

Grant took the cap to the rear of the truck, opened the back gate and let the dogs out. The two huskies, Mabel and Maud, bounded away, punched their noses into the snow and returned. Their white-masked faces and peaked ears gave them an alert, intelligent expression. Snuffy—the female golden retriever with the remarkable sense of smell—waggled over to Susan for a pat on the head, then back to Grant.

"I've been working on scenting with Snuffy," he said. "For rescuing lost hikers."

He placed the knit cap on the snow at the side of the road and pointed to it. ''Snuffy. Here, girl. Scent. Take the scent.''

''The kidnappers drove off in a Jeep. How can a dog follow the scent in a Jeep?''

''You'd be amazed by what some dogs can be trained to do.''

Apparently, Snuffy wasn't one of them. Though the loose-limbed golden retriever diligently sniffed at the cap, her first steps were into the forest.

''The Jeep did not go into the trees,'' Susan said. ''Grant, can we go?''

''Give Snuffy a minute.''

Her ex-husband seemed to be concentrating intensely—far more intensely than the dog, who was staring up through the branches of a pine and barking.

The poor, sweet animal wasn't going to find anything, but Grant watched this nonsense with rapt attention. His eyebrows lifted. He whispered under his breath. His ungloved hands moved inadvertently, urging the dog to take the scent.

Then, abruptly, he gave up. His face crumbled, and she could feel the hope draining from him.

''Snuffy! Mabel and Maud!'' Grant slapped at the side of the truck. She'd never heard him use such a sharp tone with his dogs. ''Damn it, let's go.''

Unable to witness Grant's disappointment, Susan looked away, staring instead at her little Subaru and noting a severe amount of damage to the front grill. If only she'd been able to lock the doors… If only she'd been able to throw the car in reverse and drive away, they would have escaped. Michael would be safe. He would be here with her, playing with his Game Boy, trying to reach Randy Gaylor on the cell phone. "My cell phone. Michael was playing with my cell phone."

She dug around in the front seat, finding neither cell phone nor Game Boy.

Grant stood behind her. "Now what?"

"He must have taken the phone with him. Don't you understand? That means he could call us."

"Does he know the number for Pinedale?"

She wasn't sure. "He knows the number for Mountain Rescue. Randy's number. Maybe he'll call there."

"It's a long shot," Grant said.

But it was a sliver of hope, and she clung to it desperately. "If Michael calls that number, he'll ask for Randy. Do you think we should alert him to the possibility?"

"Great idea," Grant said sarcastically as he headed toward the truck. "We shouldn't tell the cops or the FBI, but we should involve a fourteen-year-old kid. That's sheer genius, Susan."

His condescending tone set her teeth on edge, especially since she hadn't argued about wasting time with the dogs. She climbed back into the truck. "You're such a jerk."

"Lucky for you, we're divorced."

"I'm not feeling terribly lucky at the moment."

He started the engine. Easily, he backed out of the snow and headed down the road. "Okay, Susan, tell me more about the kidnappers. Do they want money?"

"Four hundred and fifty thousand dollars."

His glance was sharp. "That's a familiar number."

"I know." She remembered the exact amount of

the insurance payoff for the fire at Pinedale. "Do you think it's a coincidence?"

He came to a full stop at the main highway and leaned over the steering wheel to look both ways. "I think it's a message, but I don't understand the meaning. Earlier today, somebody reminded me that I have enemies in Rampart."

"You also have a lot of friends." Half the people in town were involved in some way with the volunteers who performed rescues. The last time Michael was up here for a visit, he'd told her about an award Grant had received. His reputation as a hero was well deserved.

"Enemies, too," he said.

If Michael had been taken by someone who wanted revenge on Grant, why ask for ransom at all? Their goal would be to hurt Grant in the most horrible way possible.

A shudder that had nothing to do with cold went through her. Though it seemed bizarre, she would have been happier if the kidnappers were merely trying to extort money from her father. In that context, the abduction would have been more like a business transaction.

Now, she couldn't help fearing that her son had been taken as part of a deranged scheme. But what? And why? Why was this happening to them?

HE CHECKED THE WINDOWS, making sure no light from the lamps would be visible from outside. Though this was the best, most clever hiding place he could think of, he checked the ammunition clips on their automatic handguns.

"Hey," Cyrus said lazily, "we aren't going to use those guns, are we?"

"We've got to be prepared." Especially after what happened with the Jeep. That hadn't been part of his plan. "Don't underestimate Grant. He's smarter than he looks."

Cyrus shook his big, stupid head. "I don't like guns."

"Too bad."

Cyrus didn't like anything. He was always complaining. It might be a real good idea, after this was over, to take one of these guns, shove it up the big man's nose and pull the trigger.

"You were right about the kid." Cyrus gestured toward the door of the adjoining room where Michael was resting comfortably. "Ever since we gave him that shot, he's been out cold."

The spoiled little brat! He'd put up a fight until they'd knocked him out. The sooner they got rid of him, the better. If little Mikey was lucky, he wouldn't have to watch his pretty mother die.

DISREGARDING SPEED limits, Grant drove fast along the main highway. The truck was headed east, toward Denver.

Coolly, Susan reminded, "Pinedale is the other way."

"I'm surprised you remember."

"Could you please put a lid on it." Why did he insist upon this petty bickering? Their son was in danger. "Like it or not, we have to work together."

"You got that right, Susan. Especially when it comes to the ransom money." He cleared his throat.

"I'm close to broke. Next week is the grand opening for Pinedale, and I've spent every nickel."

"Won't there be a restaurant? You must have kept aside some cash for paying the food suppliers."

"I'm a new account. They wanted their money up front before they'd accept the orders."

If she'd been involved at Pinedale, the suppliers wouldn't have been a problem. Not only would Susan have her father's excellent credit history to back her up, but she was also accustomed to negotiating with these people. She'd spent most of her life in the restaurant business and was, without bragging, a master chef.

Their plans for Pinedale had included a state-of-the-art kitchen with Susan in charge. She wondered if Grant had taken her suggestions or had cut corners on the restaurant end of the renovations.

She shrugged. Pinedale didn't matter. She wouldn't be there for the grand opening or at any other future time.

"Grant, will you please tell me where we're going?"

"When I stopped back at Mountain Rescue, there was a note from someone who saw a Jeep go off the Old Grange Road."

"A Jeep?" Excitement welled inside her. "Do you think it's the kidnappers? Was anyone hurt? Did it say anything about—"

"I don't know anything other than that a woman who lives up here called in a minor car accident to Mountain Rescue because she couldn't reach anybody at the sheriff's office."

He took a right at the turnoff beside the Old Grange Hall.

Susan's heart beat faster as they followed the winding road into a narrow canyon. A steep wall on the east side kept the entire area in shadow, and the accumulated snowfall mounted in high drifts.

Though she still believed they should follow the kidnappers' instructions, she couldn't help hoping that they would find Michael and bring him to safety. The sooner the better. "What are we looking for? What part of the road?"

"Don't know. The woman's name was Adrian Walker. Look for her mailbox."

Most of the cabins in this area were set back from the two-lane road, almost hidden in the snow-laden conifers, but the mailboxes were roadside, where the Rampart postmistress could easily make her drops. The boxes showed a distinct individuality, painted with names and designs that meant something to the residents. One row of three mailboxes boasted a "Crowe," a "Fox Family," and "The Bayers."

Susan looked overhead. The sun was falling lower in the sky. Minutes were passing as quickly as sand through an hourglass. "Hurry, Grant. We don't have much time."

"I know."

In a series of hairpin turns, the road ascended, then led straight along a cliff with no guardrail. The drop-off was steep and treacherous, plummeting sixty feet or more. She shivered as she peered over the edge. It seemed unlikely that the kidnappers would bother with seat belts.

The road went down, leveling out a bit.

"There it is!" Susan pointed to a fire-engine-red mailbox. "Walker."

Grant slowed his truck.

Their careful surveillance was unnecessary. They couldn't miss the Jeep. The tail end was only a few yards off the shoulder. The nose was wedged tightly between two pine trees.

Susan was out of the truck before it had completely stopped. Recklessly, she charged down the steep, snowy embankment to the Jeep, running headlong into the rear end. When she stepped away from the vehicle, her gloves and the front of her parka were imprinted with frozen muck.

"I think this is the same Jeep," she called to Grant. "The one the kidnappers were driving."

Peering around the vehicle, she noted the scrape along the rear fender, marked with paint from her Subaru. There was a crack in the windshield. The front hood had buckled. If the downward slide of the Jeep hadn't been stopped by the two pine trees, it might have careened another thirty feet into deep forest.

She stared down the steep cliff and thought of Michael. He must have been terrified during this accident. Her son was always so cautious about fastening his seat belt. He checked her speed more frequently than a police radar, advising her when she wasn't following legal limits. Had he been injured? Was he all right?

Grant joined her at the rear of the Jeep. He hunkered down and wiped clean the place where there should have been a license plate. There was nothing but mud and snow. "I'll bet it's stolen," he said.

"But the Jeep has to be registered," she said. "Even if it was stolen, there might be a clue. Isn't there some other way we can find out who owns it?"

"We'll try." But his expression wasn't encouraging. "Do you notice anything weird about this accident site?"

"Just tell me, Grant."

"You said you wanted to start thinking. To be rational."

She was thinking of Michael. His fear. The possibility that he'd been hurt. But if she indulged those concerns, they would feed upon themselves and become obstacles. Grant was right. She needed to be logical and sensible.

"No footprints," he said. "I see your tracks in the snow—and mine—but there's no other sign that anybody climbed up from here."

But the Jeep had gone off the road and crashed into the trees. "How can that be?"

"I'm not sure." He gestured toward the front of the Jeep. "You look through the glove compartment. See if there's anything inside that might give us an idea where to start."

"Is it safe to go inside the car? My weight won't cause it to dislodge, will it?"

"You'll be fine," he said.

As if he cared one whit about what might happen to her. Grant would probably be thrilled if she plummeted down the cliff. If she were out of the way, he would be relieved of his child-support payments, and he would have Michael with him full time.

Their court fight over custody hadn't been amicable. Grant had insisted that Denver was too far from Rampart for him to see his son as often as he wanted. Never mind that her employment was in Denver, as well as her support system of family and friends. All Grant had cared about was his own convenience. At one point, when their battling was most intense, she'd even feared that he might kidnap Michael himself.

Would he? Was it possible?

A chill wind touched her throat as she watched her ex-husband surefootedly circle toward the front of the car. Could he have been responsible for stealing Michael?

He glared back at her. "What's your problem?"

"Nothing."

Now wasn't the time to voice her suspicions. They were working together as partners.

"Come on, Susan. Hurry up. If you're afraid to go into the Jeep, I'll do it."

If he made the search, he could hide the evidence. These suspicions seemed ludicrous, but she couldn't help it. Once, she'd trusted him—and he'd torn her life to shreds.

Mentally, she pieced together the meager facts. The kidnappers insisted they wait for the call at Pinedale, and being at the hotel was definitely to Grant's advantage. He'd said he wouldn't call the sheriff. Grant had known to come here, to this exact point on the road. Had a call really been made to Mountain Rescue?

"Susan? What's wrong?"

Stiffly she responded, "Never mind, Grant. I'll search in the Jeep."

"Terrific."

Slowly he looked away from her and shook his head. At one time, he'd been able to read every thought that danced through her constantly active mind. They'd been linked on a deep, almost-primal level. Now, he couldn't guess what motivated her. They were as distant as strangers.

While Susan dug around inside the car, he went to the hood and looked underneath. The soldered metal tag that should have been permanent identification for the Jeep's registration had been removed. Grant rubbed at the blank space above the engine block. The smell of gasoline was heavy, and a cursory examination showed a ruptured hose. A trickle of gas marked the engine block. Car trouble. The kidnappers' getaway had been thwarted by car trouble.

Stepping back, he studied the vehicle. The two trees that had stopped it were slender pines. If the Jeep had been going at any speed when it went off the road, it would have plowed them down.

Susan, looking harried, shouted to him. "There's nothing inside. No papers. No discarded wrappers from fast-food joints. No notes. Nothing."

Her voice trembled on the last word. She sounded close to tears. Understandably. But he sure as hell didn't need for her to start weeping. It wouldn't help Michael. "Let's go back up to the road."

Easily, he ascended the steep, snowy embankment. This was his country, his land. At one time, Susan had been a part of this world, walking confidently at his side. Now, she stumbled over the rocks like a flatlander. He said nothing until she was standing beside him.

"Here's what I think happened," he explained. "They were leaking gas. It didn't look like they were going to get much farther, so they sabotaged the Jeep."

"How?"

"They got out and pushed it off the road."

"That explains why there were no footprints leading back to the road."

"Right," he said. "They probably hoped the Jeep would crash all the way down, deep into the forest where it wouldn't have been found for weeks."

She frowned. "But why?"

"They didn't need it anymore. I'd guess the Jeep is stolen. The identification number is gone and so are the plates. They must have had another car nearby."

"Or else they're holed up around here somewhere," she said.

Though he doubted that the kidnappers would be stupid enough to leave the Jeep in plain sight near their hideout, he conceded the possibility. "We should check around. At least, try to find this Adrian Walker who reported the Jeep."

"But quickly," she reminded him.

"I know, Susan."

She must think he was a moron, incapable of holding a simple thought in his mind. Looking away from her, Grant scanned the snow-covered terrain of the canyon. From where they stood, he could see a neatly kept cabin that was only a little way back from the road. The front door was painted blue. The porch had been shoveled. There was an attached garage, and the snow was worn down where the tires had made ruts.

Together they crossed the road. When he rapped on the door, he glanced over at Susan. She'd gotten messy exploring the Jeep, and the smudge across her cheek sparked an urge to reach over and wipe her face. But he held back. His tenderness would be misinterpreted. If he touched her, she would shove him away.

A bright-eyed older lady opened the door. She wore jeans, a thermal undershirt and a plaid flannel shirt. Her taffy-white braids were wrapped around her head.

Grant said, "Are you Adrian Walker?"

"That's right."

"You called in the Jeep accident to Mountain Rescue, and I'm here to check it out."

"Come on inside. The open door lets out all my heat."

They entered a cozy front room. In the late afternoon, the lamp beside a comfortable-looking chair was already lit, and a fire blazed cheerily on the moss-rock hearth.

Grant got right to the point. "Did you see the accident?"

"No, sir. I was out doing my marketing so I'd be all stocked up before the blizzard hits tomorrow, and I saw the Jeep when I got back. Didn't look to be much of an accident, but I thought I ought to call it in all the same. Couldn't get through to the sheriff, and I don't trust those phone-message machines, so I called Mountain Rescue."

"Do you recognize the Jeep?"

"Doesn't belong to any of my nearby neighbors," she said. "But I don't know everybody who lives along this road. Not anymore."

"What about the cabin a little farther up?" Susan asked. "I saw smoke coming from his chimney."

"I don't much care for him," she said crisply. "He drinks a bit. Summer days, he sits on his porch and shoots at the tree squirrels. Kind of squirrelly himself, if you ask me. His name is O'Dell."

"Bart O'Dell?" Grant questioned.

"That's him." She squinted up at him. "You're

the young fellow who's been working on Pinedale, aren't you?"

"Yes, ma'am."

"I'm glad for what you're doing. I remember Pinedale from when I was a little girl." Her weathered features lifted in an easy smile. "It was 1928, and my family went to a fancy party there. That big hotel was a fine sight. All lit up and shining. Ladies in long dresses and the men in suits. Oh, my, it was swell."

"I'd be honored for you to visit Pinedale," he said. "Come in the afternoon and ask for me, Grant Richardson. We'll have tea."

"Thank you." She smiled sweetly. "It's a date, Grant."

When they were again outside, hiking around the curve to the next cabin, Susan muttered, "You haven't changed a bit. Still charming the ladies."

"Oh, yeah. I'm hot stuff with the over-seventy crowd."

"You do okay with the younger women, too," she said. "Anybody special?"

"No. And you?"

"I don't have time between managing the south Colorado Boulevard restaurant, keeping track of my father and taking Michael back and forth to preschool and day care."

"How's he doing in preschool?"

"He's wonderful with numbers. I know every mother says this about her son, but he might be gifted."

"Of course he's gifted," Grant said. "You're keeping him active with other stuff, aren't you?"

"Guy stuff? Athletic stuff?" She rolled her eyes.

"Don't worry, I'm not turning your son into a sissy. Michael is joining a soccer team this spring."

"Soccer, huh?"

Grant was pleased and, at the same time, disappointed. He wished he could be there with his son, attending his soccer games, practicing with him on weekends. He could teach him how to throw, how to kick, how to run.

In the noblest part of Grant's mind, he wanted the best for his son and his ex-wife. He hoped Susan would find another man so Michael would grow up with a masculine influence. But he hated the idea that someone else would take his place.

At the base of the hill, there was a weathered shed, big enough to be a garage. Behind it, a worn footpath led up a steep hillside to a small cabin that perched only a few yards back from a retaining wall. Unlike the tidy premises belonging to Adrian Walker, there was a lot of clutter around O'Dell's place.

Grant cracked the door of the shed and looked inside. Junk and tools lined the walls. Against the rear wall there was a small supply of firewood with a rusting ax propped beside it. The vacant space in the middle suggested that this shed was used to garage a car or a small truck.

"Do you know this guy?" Susan asked.

"He did some carpentry work for me at Pinedale."

"You don't like him," she said. "I can tell by your voice."

"He's rude, crude and not a skilled worker. After two days on the job, I fired his sorry behind."

Bart O'Dell was another name to add to his list of enemies, and Grant didn't like the coincidence of finding him living near the kidnappers' Jeep. He hiked up the steep pathway to the front porch. In spite of the smoke from the chimney, the cabin was dark inside.

The front door swung open wide. Framed within was a scrawny old man in ragged long johns, steel-toed boots and a two-day growth of grizzled beard. He leveled a shotgun barrel at Grant's chest.

Chapter Four

Grant could smell O'Dell's whiskey breath from four feet away. The man looked as though he'd been on a three-day bender. There was no telling what this old drunk might do. "Put down the gun, O'Dell."

"I got a right to shoot trespassers."

"We'll leave as soon as you answer a couple of questions. What do you know about the Jeep accident down the road?"

"Don't know nothing. Don't care."

"Did you see what happened? Did you see who was driving?"

His rheumy eyes shifted from Grant to Susan. "Who's this?"

Without flinching, she held out her hand toward him. Her gesture reminded Grant of the way she dealt with his dogs. Reach out and let them sniff around until they accept you.

In a clear voice, she said, "I'm Susan Richardson."

He licked the corners of his mouth. "The ex-wife, eh? Oh, yes. Yes, indeedy. I'll tell you this, little lady, you're too damn pretty to be with Grant."

Grant hated the way O'Dell was leering at her. "That's enough."

"Seems to me like you'd better not take that high-and-mighty tone with me, Grant. I'm on the business end of this here rifle."

"Speaking of guns," Susan said. She lightly touched the steel barrel of his shotgun and tried to push it aside. "Let's put this one away."

He swiveled his aim so the bore pointed at her. "I reckon you wouldn't be half so pretty if I blew a big hole in your midsection."

Her tension was apparent in her stiff posture and the slight tremble of her hands. Yet she kept her voice soft and cajoling. "You wouldn't really shoot me, would you, Mr. O'Dell?"

"Probably not, sweetheart. But there's them who would."

"Like who?" Grant asked. Did this guy know something?

O'Dell glanced furtively and whispered, "Can't say."

"Can't or won't?" The distinction was lost on O'Dell, who pulled a frown and kept eyeballing Susan. Grant clarified, "Are you trying to warn us?"

"I ain't talking." He waved the shotgun between them. "Get off my land."

"Don't play games with me." Grant didn't have the patience to deal with this old drunk. Time was passing too quickly. The hour of investigation was running out. "Is someone after Susan?"

"A pretty thing like her? Betcha lots of men are after her. Hell, if I was twenty years younger, I might—"

"Is Susan in danger?"

For an instant, there was clarity in his gaze. "An

eye for an eye. A tooth for a tooth. A death for a death. A single red rose will mark her grave."

Susan gasped. "What does that mean, Mr. O'Dell? Should I be afraid?"

"Hell, yes. We should all be afraid."

"Of what?" Grant demanded.

O'Dell shrugged. His cranky stupidity fell back into place. "Hell, why should you listen to me? I'm just a tired old drunk. Sometimes people tell me things. They think I don't remember."

"Did someone talk to you about Susan?"

His tongue poked around inside his cheek, distorting his face. "I got nothing more to say."

"Can we come inside?" Susan asked. "It's cold out here."

"Why do you want to come in?" His upper lip curled in a sly sneer. "You think I got something to hide?"

Obviously Bart O'Dell had secrets. He was out on his porch, waving a shotgun, protecting something that was stashed in the dark lair of his cabin. Michael? Though it hadn't really occurred to him before, Grant wondered if the old man was involved in the kidnapping. Was he holding Michael inside his filthy hovel?

In a way, this was a brilliant hideout—the last place Grant would have thought to look. He had no use for O'Dell, no interest in him. Bart O'Dell was a nonentity, less important than a spider he would crush under his heel. But spiders could bite. "Step aside, O'Dell."

"Why?"

"Because I'm coming inside to take a look around."

The tip of his gun barrel jabbed into the center of

Grant's parka. "I'm within my rights to shoot you for trespassing. Now, get the hell out of here."

"I'll be back," Grant said. "Be careful, O'Dell. I might be back with the sheriff to see what you've got in there."

"If I am hiding something—and I'm not saying that I am—it might be buried under ten feet of snow before you get back here."

Was he talking about Michael? Grant couldn't stand here passively for one more second. With no thought for his own safety, he caught hold of the rifle and tore it from O'Dell's shaky hands.

With one swift motion, he tossed the weapon over the edge of the retaining wall that kept the dilapidated house perched on its cliff. Then he turned back to the scrawny old man, who stood gaping in the doorway.

"O'Dell, you have three seconds to get the hell out of my way. One. Two—"

"You can't do this!" He appealed to Susan. "Make him stop. He can't come in here unless I say so."

"What are you hiding, O'Dell?"

"Nothing. I swear."

"Three," Grant said.

He feinted to the left, then to the right, and pushed the old man aside.

Inside, the one-room cabin was disgusting. The smoke-stained walls were a dingy gray. Underfoot, there was the crunching of old dirt and discarded newspaper. Even the fire on the hearth appeared dirty. There was a half-empty whiskey bottle and a mason-jar glass in a small cleared space on a wood table piled high with discarded junk mail and used plates.

"Upstairs," Susan said, pointing to an open stairway that was little more than a ladder.

"No," O'Dell said. "You can't go up there."

Grant wished he hadn't thrown away the shotgun. If the kidnappers were up there, he would be an idiot to charge up those stairs unarmed. But that was exactly what he had to do.

He inhaled deeply and thought of Michael. At a run, he burst up the stairs into a poorly lit loft area with a low ceiling. A mattress and bedclothes were lumped in one corner. Other clothes were strewn across a beat-up dresser. There was no sign of Michael or anyone else.

Susan followed. Quickly, she made a search of the closet and pawed through the filthy blankets. "I don't think Michael was here. I don't see anything."

"I do," Grant said.

There was a stack of tools beside the stairs, including an electrical circular saw that Grant had been missing for a long time, probably ever since O'Dell had worked for him.

He picked up the tool. "This is what he was hiding. It belongs to me."

Susan sighed. "Is that all?"

"Afraid so."

"For a minute, I thought he might actually have Michael here. In this mess."

"I thought so, too. Especially when he started spouting that eye-for-an-eye stuff."

"So sad," Susan said. "This place smells like despair."

It seemed to Grant that she was willing to be understanding about everyone. Everyone but him.

"Let me go down the stairs first," Grant said, "in case O'Dell thinks he's going to ambush us."

He descended quickly with the heavy saw in his hand. It made a formidable weapon, which O'Dell must have realized, because he sat quietly behind the table, cradling his whiskey bottle like a baby. "You owed me, Grant. You never should have fired me. I'm a good carpenter. So, I figured you owed me. That's why I took your saw."

"I'm taking it back," Grant said.

"Fine with me. I don't need it, anyway. Sven Dahlberg provides tools for his workers."

"Have you been working for Sven?"

"That's right. He's employing a lot of the local men to work on his shiny new condo development. It's going to put Pinedale to shame."

"Who else works for Sven?"

"Everybody. He don't pay as much as you, but it's regular, and he ain't so picky."

That was an understatement. From what Grant had seen of Sven's condos, the ten-unit buildings were prefab monstrosities. "So, how do you get back and forth to work?"

"In my truck."

"Where is it?" Grant asked. "Before we came up here, we checked in your shed at the bottom of the hill, and there wasn't a truck parked in there."

"By damn!" The old man staggered out the door of his cabin and hiked down the hill with startling agility. He whipped open the garage door and cursed. Like Rumpelstiltskin, he jumped up and down. A jet stream of O'Dell's loud obscenities echoed through the chilly air of the canyon.

When Susan and Grant joined him, he stated the obvious. "Some cussed varmint swiped my truck."

"How long has it been missing?"

Pacing in a tight circle, he waved his arms over his head. "What am I going to do? I need my truck."

"How long has it been gone?" Grant repeated.

"Let's see.... I didn't leave the house today. Come to think on it, I didn't leave yesterday, neither." He kicked the side of the garage. "Whoever took it is in for a surprise. There ain't hardly no gas."

This was good news for Grant; if the kidnappers had taken O'Dell's truck, they wouldn't get too far. "What does your truck look like?"

"It's a pea-green Toyota. Fifteen years ago, she was brand-new."

He didn't need to add that the truck was on its last legs; Grant could assume as much. "You'd better call the sheriff and report it missing."

"Doggone right, I will. And if my rifle is messed up, I'm sending you a bill, Grant."

"You do that."

Back in the truck, finally headed toward Pinedale, Susan turned to him and said, "Quite possibly, that was the stupidest interrogation and assault I can imagine."

"Thanks, dear," he drawled. "I rose to the occasion, dealing with a criminal mastermind like O'Dell."

"What if Michael had been in that cabin? Did you really think you'd save him by throwing away the rifle and running up the stairs like Rambo?"

"It was better than standing by. You weren't exactly making great progress by being nice to him."

Her voice was sharp. "What if the kidnappers had

been holed up there, waiting with guns? They could have shot Michael.''

He knew she was right. In his rescue experience, he'd learned that the most immediate response wasn't always the best.

"You could have gotten him killed," she said. "And yourself, too."

Then she subsided, leaning back in the seat and staring through the windshield, shifting positions to get comfortable. She needed comforting, but she wouldn't accept it from him.

Under her breath, she muttered, "When will you stop?"

"Stop what?"

"Stop trying to be a damned hero."

They rode for a long distance in uneasy silence. Accusations, past and present, hung between them.

Finally Susan asked, "Are we making a mistake by not telling the police? They might be able to search the area."

"A normal police department could do that," Grant said, "but every vehicle in the Rampart Sheriff's office was busy this afternoon with the broken-down school bus. Maybe the Colorado State Patrol could help. We could call them."

"It's a possibility. Let's wait until we hear from the kidnappers."

He nodded in agreement. Right now, the kidnappers had a big problem. They were cruising around in a truck that was known to belong to Bart O'Dell. A truck with no gas. When they realized they had a problem with the Jeep, they must have figured they could come up here and swipe O'Dell's truck without the old man noticing.

Grant didn't like the direction in which his conclusions were leading. It seemed that the kidnappers had knowledge of Bart O'Dell and his bender. If so, it meant they were locals.

He explained his logic to Susan, concluding by saying, "If they know O'Dell, they must live around here. Maybe they were on their way to another cabin on that road."

"Do you know the people who live up there?"

"I can't think of anybody. You know how it is, Susan. I meet people in town or at Pinedale, but I don't know where their cabins are."

He needed to go through his list of enemies again. If he counted all the grudges, tabulated each and every angry moment, there could be a long roster. There were people, like Donny Evanston and Doc, who hated him because of the fire. Others were envious over Pinedale or, like Sven, wanted the hotel for their own. And there were people, like O'Dell, who hated Grant because he pushed his work crews and demanded no less than perfection.

Now that Pinedale was complete, he wondered if the job had been worth the cost. Almost single-handedly, he'd built a hotel. And he'd destroyed his family.

By FOUR-THIRTY, DUSK had settled over the Rampart valley, and the phones at Slade's Adventures and the volunteer Mountain Rescue were quiet.

Randy Gaylor hunched over his algebra textbook, staring blankly at pages of formulas and coefficients.

"Tough assignment?" his mom asked.

Randy nodded. He wanted to tell her about Michael's kidnapping. But he couldn't. He owed it to Grant to keep quiet.

In the back of his mind, he remembered the last time he'd seen Michael. Not that long ago, near Christmas. Michael had wanted to show Randy his brand-new Saturn Patrol wristwatch. Like always, Randy had called him ''little dude.'' Then he'd taken off to go snowboarding with his buds.

''Randy?''

''Huh?''

His mom was standing right next to him. She had that ''mother'' look—like she wanted to muss up his hair and give him a hug. But he was too old for that stuff. ''Are you okay, Randy?''

''Yeah, sure.''

If he told her, what could she do? She would just get freaked. He chewed on his lower lip to keep from talking.

''I need to go back to the house for a minute,'' she said. ''Can you keep an eye on the phones for me?''

''Okay.''

She stuck her arms into her parka and pulled her long braid out over the collar. She was pretty, and Randy liked that she was. It made him proud. He didn't know why his mom wasn't dating anybody, like Hal Haverly, the rancher who helped Randy with 4-H stuff.

''I'll be right back,'' she said.

She'd been gone twenty minutes when the Mountain Rescue telephone rang.

HALF A MILE PAST the town, Grant took the turnoff that led to Pinedale. In the fading light, the hotel loomed before them. Though Grant liked to think of it as a "chateau," the architecture was a jumble of different styles. Susan had once called it "Primitive Victorian."

The foundation, which rose three feet from the ground, was of stone masonry, as were the seven fireplaces; but the walls were wood siding, painted a glistening white. The ornate cornices above the front section and all the trim were charcoal gray. The third story was a series of dormers where Grant had hidden solar panels to help with the cost of heating this behemoth.

In front, there was covered parking for forty cars, as well as seven separate, enclosed garages that went with the suites. Grant kept the approach cleared with his snowplow, and the asphalt showed through on the circular drive at the entrance.

In his opinion, the renovation had turned out well, especially the interior. Would Susan approve? When she'd left him, she'd cursed the hotel and all it stood for. She called it his "obsession"—the giant wedge that had driven them apart—and she had sworn never to set foot inside again.

He parked outside the front door. The interior lights, on a timer, were shining through sparkling, triple-paned windows. "I'll leave the truck out here," he said. "If the kidnappers are watching, they'll know we're doing what they told us."

"Yes," she said tersely. "That would be best."

He opened the back of his truck and let the dogs run wild. Later, he would take them around to the fenced enclosure and doghouses at the rear of the hotel.

As Susan climbed the four broad steps to the front entry, he wished he could have carried her over the threshold, and he hoped she would gaze upon his efforts with approval.

He unlocked the door and held it open for her.

The front desk was carved mahogany—the original piece, painstakingly refinished. Hardwood floors, polished to a high gloss, spanned the entry. Meeting rooms on either side of the lobby stood waiting behind curtained French doors.

Though Grant wasn't good with plants, Susan had told him a long time ago that foliage was the easiest decor, and he'd taken her advice. There was an abundance of greenery. The artwork on the walls, selected with great personal care and an eye on the budget, included a couple of retouched paintings that had been stored in the attic of Pinedale.

The portrait of Susan by Johnny Rosewood had a place of honor behind the front desk. Grant liked the idea that guests and visitors to Pinedale would be welcomed by Susan's laughing hazel eyes and tousled hair.

He closed the door. "Well?"

"Oh, Grant." When she faced him, her lips trembled in a tenuous smile. "It's everything we dreamed it could be."

"HEY, LITTLE DUDE." Randy immediately recognized Michael's voice on the telephone. "What's up?"

"My daddy. Is he around?"

Was Michael still with the kidnappers or had everything gotten sorted out? Randy didn't know what to say. "I can look for your dad."

"Okay. He's supposed to pick me up."

He didn't sound scared, and that was cool. If Michael wasn't freaked, Randy didn't want to make him feel that way. He swallowed the strangled feeling in his throat. "Where are you waiting, little dude?"

"All by myself. In bed. I got a Saturn Patrol video."

"Is your mom around?"

"Nope."

But where was he? Randy figured he might get a fix on Michael's location if he could get the little guy to describe some landmarks. "Hey, Michael, is there a window in your room?"

"It's kinda dark."

"Can you take a look outside?"

"Okay."

Randy heard shuffling sounds as the five-year-old boy moved around. "Michael? What do you see?"

"Snow and trees."

"Anything else?" Randy asked.

"I dunno."

Michael sounded kind of dopey, and Randy asked, "Are you okay, little dude?"

"These two guys gave me a shot. In my butt."

The kidnappers must have drugged him. That was bad news with a little kid like Michael. "Are you sleepy?"

"A lot sleepy," he said. "I only waked up one time until now."

"The last time you woke up, did you see anything?"

"Elephant Rock." He made a sniffling noise that turned into a yawn. "I want my dad. And my mom."

"These guys," Randy said, "they're not hurting you or anything, are they?"

"They're dumb."

Randy tried to turn his questions into a game. "If

you had to guess where you were, what would you say.''

"I'm sleepy, Randy."

"Don't hang up, little dude. I really want to talk."

"Night, night. Don't let the bedbugs bite."

The line went dead, and Randy shook the telephone receiver in his fist, wishing the dial tone would go away and he could talk to Michael again.

As his mother came through the door, Randy carefully replaced the receiver on the hook.

SUSAN MARVELED AT the beauty of Pinedale. When she'd left Grant, the renovation had been mostly sketches and imagination. He'd accomplished so much. Though the lobby was shy on furniture, the decor created an atmosphere of charm and careful attention to detail.

She stood at the front desk and indulged in a prideful study of the portrait of herself. In it, she was laughing, her head thrown back. Her long black hair flew around her face in tangles, and her cheeks glowed with health. Though the technique was crude, the artist had captured a bright, optimistic spirit, and the painting brought a smile to her lips. It was hard to believe that she'd ever been so carefree and happy.

"Do you like it?" Grant asked.

She nodded. The portrait made her feel special, as if she were someone grand and important and very much beloved. By Grant? How could that be?

"I had it commissioned," he said.

"By the same artist who did the portrait of Rachel at Doc's house?"

"Johnny Rosewood. He's good, isn't he? He copied it from a photo, but I talked to him a lot when he was painting, and he added details from the things I told him.''

A radiant warmth unfolded within her. The memories he added to this painting must have been happy ones. At some level, he still cared for her. "Oh, Grant. It's beautiful.''

"I took that photo two months before you gave birth. I loved the way you looked when you were pregnant. You had this amazing glow. You were so incredible then.''

And now? Her short-lived pleasure faded as she turned away from the portrait. Slowly, her gaze lowered to the telephone switchboard behind the front desk. "Were there any calls?''

"I'll play back the messages.''

The kidnappers? Tensely, she waited while five recorded messages played—all were business related, pertaining to his grand opening next weekend.

Though disappointed, Susan was glad they hadn't missed a contact from the kidnappers. She didn't want to do anything that might set them off. The smaller man—the one who had done most of the talking—had a bad temper.

"I should put the dogs away," Grant said. "Get them fed and bedded down for the night. Want to come with me?''

"I'd like to see the dogs, especially Pyrite." Her gaze riveted on the phones. "But I should stay here. In case they call.''

After quick instructions on how to use the switchboard, he headed for the front door.

Susan settled herself in a swivel chair behind the desk. To her right was a closed door marked Manager, but the switchboard area was its own separate office.

There were notepads for messages, a standing file and a calendar where Grant had circled today and written, "Michael—2:00 p.m.—Mtn Resc." The small digital clock beside the files had clicked off only one minute before the main office phone jangled.

Startled, she jumped and grabbed the receiver, forgetting all Grant's instructions for using the headset, turning on the recorder and operating the switchboard.

"Hello?"

"About time you got there, Susan. I called once before and got an answering machine."

She recognized the voice of the kidnapper and waved to Grant, who raced back to the desk. Into the phone, she asked, "How's Michael? Is he all right?"

"Don't worry about the kid. He's sound asleep."

"I want to talk to him," she said.

Grant stood behind her. His hand rested on her shoulder and she laced her trembling fingers through his.

"No talking," the kidnapper said. "Is Grant with you?"

"Yes. I've done everything the way you said. About Michael, is he—"

"Did you get the money?"

"I haven't had a chance," she said. "It's a lot to—"

"Get it," he ordered. "By tomorrow morning at ten o'clock. I'll call to tell you where to make the drop."

"You've got to be reasonable," she said. "I don't know how we can get that much money so quickly."

"Come on, Susan. Your ex has money. So does your daddy. Pete Falcone is a big man."

"His restaurants are all the way into Denver. That's a five-hour drive from here. I need more time."

"So you can contact the cops? No way, honey. You get the money—four hundred and fifty thousand—by tomorrow at ten. Unless you want little Mikey to have an accident."

"Damn you! I can't—"

The phone went dead in her hand.

Her eyelids squeezed shut against the terror and pain. White-knuckled, her grip on Grant's hand tightened.

"What did he say?" he asked. "What does the bastard want?"

"The ransom. By tomorrow at ten." She felt battered, beaten into a tight corner from which there was no escape. "He told me to ask my father for money, even mentioned him by name."

"So, the kidnapper knows your father," Grant said. "Maybe this is somebody who followed you from town. That would explain how they picked out your new car. None of the locals would know about the Subaru."

"But they'd know me," she said.

"How? You didn't recognize them. How would they know what you look like?"

"That." She ripped her hand away from him and pointed to the portrait. "That's how they'd know me. And look at your calendar. Right here in plain sight. It says where you're supposed to meet Michael, and the time."

Unable to stand still, she leaped from the chair and paced across the lobby. Her boot heels echoed like thunder on the hardwood floors. She hadn't meant to yell at him. "Listen, Grant, I agree with you. It's important to figure out who the kidnappers are. Or who they're working for. We need every advantage."

"I'm glad you can finally see it that way."

"There's a lot that I see," she said. "And I think it's almost impossible to figure this out."

"Nothing is impossible."

Brutally honest, she continued, "I see Donny Evanston, who hates you. Bart O'Dell, who hates you. And this Sven person you keep mentioning. So many people have a motive for hurting you."

"But who among them is insane enough to kidnap a child?" He came around the counter and leaned against it, his arms folded across his broad chest. "What about you, Susan? O'Dell hinted that somebody is after you. Maybe you ought to make up an enemy list of your own."

"Well, that won't take long. As far as I know, there's only one person who hates me." Her gaze riveted to his face. "That's you, Grant."

"I've never hated you."

"You put me through hell. After the fire, my life was a living hell. Day in and day out. I've lost count of the nights when I'd lie beside you, praying you'd touch me. I was desperate. I wanted you to hold me."

"I needed time."

"It was a year. You barely spoke to me." She'd given him every chance to recover. She'd forgiven and forgiven until there was no forbearance left. Only bitterness and endless hurt. "For a whole year, you ignored me and Michael, except to complain."

"I never stopped loving you."

"All that mattered to you was Pinedale. And the fire."

"How could I forget the fire? It was my fault that Rachel died."

"It was an accident!" she shouted. "A propane tank exploded in the kitchen. The insurance company investigated. They said it wasn't anybody's fault."

Slowly he came toward her. He seemed to be measuring his steps. "I'll only say this once, Susan."

"Forget it, Grant. There's nothing you can—"

"I'm sorry." He took both her hands in his. His eyes compelled her with a magnetic blue light. His voice was a barely audible whisper. "For the pain I've caused you, I'm sorry. I drove you away, and I apologize for that. I'm sorry for Michael, growing up without a father. I'm so damned sorry for everything."

She collapsed into his arms, trembling fiercely, wishing he could be the man she had once loved with all her heart. But they couldn't erase the past. His apology wouldn't compensate, and there was no tenderness in their embrace. They clung together, united by fear.

Helplessly, she said, "We have to do what the kidnappers say, or else they'll hurt him."

He stroked her back. His touch was so familiar. The outdoorsy scent of him filled her nostrils. She'd missed this special closeness. And yet, she couldn't allow herself to be seduced into believing in their love. It was gone. Irrevocably over and done with.

She stepped away from him. "I guess we need to think about getting the ransom money."

"I guess so."

"We have to go to my father," she said.

"Can we get the money without telling him about the kidnapping?"

"We have to." If Susan informed her hot-tempered father that his only grandchild had been kidnapped, he would mobilize the National Guard. "Somehow, I'll convince him to give me the money without telling him why I need it. I guess I should call him first."

She glanced at the clock. It was five-thirty, almost dinner hour. Her father would be at one of the restaurants, probably the downtown eatery. That was his favorite.

But Susan didn't want to call him there. Pete Falcone was always distracted at work—yelling at the busboys, cajoling the chefs and schmoozing with the customers. He always had a new joke for his regulars, and the fact that his grandson had been kidnapped didn't make for a funny punch line.

Instead, she called her parents' home phone. The answering machine picked up, and she heard her mother's soft voice. "You've reached the Falcones. I'm so sorry we can't come to the phone...."

She truly did sound sorry. Carolyn Falcone was the most honest woman Susan had ever known. Mama had always been a quiet figure, the woman who stood steadfastly behind her temperamental husband and her five children.

In many ways, Susan wanted to be like her. When she and Grant had first embarked on the renovation of Pinedale, she'd thought that her destiny was to be like her mother, devoting most of her life to the support of her man.

On the answering-machine recording, Carolyn Falcone concluded, "Please leave a message."

Susan hung up without speaking and looked over at Grant. "This is something I need to do in person.

We'd better get started if we're going to drive all the way to Denver and back.''

"You've got to be joking. We don't have time to drive back and forth. In case you hadn't noticed, there's a blizzard on the way. We could get stuck or stranded.''

He was right, of course. "What do you suggest?''

"Your father could wire money to the bank.''

Though a wire transfer seemed like a rational solution, Pete Falcone wasn't a reasonable man, especially when it came to money. When Susan was a teenager, it had taken two months of arguing to convince her father to raise her allowance from five dollars a week to eight. How could she call him up and ask for four hundred and fifty thousand dollars? Without even offering an explanation?

"No way,'' she said, shaking her head. "Don't you remember what my father is like? He's more volatile than Mount St. Helens.''

"I don't see what difference it's going to make whether you're there or here.''

"I can look him in the eye and negotiate. I can't let him erupt and tell somebody about the kidnapping. I won't take that chance.''

Susan wished for an easier way, but gathering the ransom would be complicated. The banks were already closed, and she didn't want to risk waiting until tomorrow at nine to start this transaction. If her father couldn't put his hands on enough cash, she'd need to find another source tonight.

Firmly, she said, "We're going to have to drive.''

"Maybe not.''

Grant needed to do his part. He already felt inadequate about not being able to pay the ransom from his own cash reserves. The least he could do was solve their transportation problem.

Suspiciously, she said, "What do you mean?"

"We can fly. I'll contact Jack Slade and work something out."

"Perfect," she said. "Let's go."

"First let me get the dogs taken care of. Then we'll worry about getting a plane or a chopper."

He strode out the front door into the early evening. The sun had fled, but the black cloak of night had not yet fallen over the valley. Overhead, the clouds portending tomorrow's blizzard had moved into place. There was a bite in the air.

"Snuffy!" he called. "Mabel and Maud!"

Though his six Siberian husky sled dogs and two golden retrievers were well-behaved, the opening of Pinedale would be difficult for them. They were accustomed to having the run of the land. After the hotel was operational, the dogs would have to spend more time confined to their pen.

Mabel and Maud bounded up to him. Their pink tongues lolled in the corner of their mouths, which seemed fixed in mischievous grins.

"Snuffy!"

The golden retriever was nowhere in sight. Usually he didn't worry much about the dogs disappearing for a while. They would always turn up. But now Grant was in a hurry.

He spied Snuffy at the end of the parking lot beside the farthest of the enclosed garages. Snuffy was digging in the snow. Must have found a bone. Grant called to her, "Snuffy!"

The dog looked up suddenly, as if she'd heard her master's voice for the first time.

"Come on, girl!"

She pawed once again at the snow, then abandoned her quest and came loping toward him, ears flying.

"Grant!" Susan was at the front door. "Come quickly."

"What is it?"

"You have a phone call from Randy Gaylor. He said he could only talk to you."

Chapter Five

As Grant rushed through the front door of Pinedale, Susan held the door for him. "Hurry," she whispered. "Please, hurry."

He had the impression that her voice was suffocated in her throat. "Take a deep breath, Susan."

"I'm fine." But he could feel the trembling in her hands as she pushed him toward the switchboard. "Randy's waiting. I know he's got news about Michael. I just know it. Michael must have called him on the cell phone. Finally we're going to hear something."

Behind the registration desk, Grant sank into the chair beside the telephone switchboard. He yanked off his gloves and picked up the telephone receiver. "Hi, Randy. What is it?"

"I've got something to tell you. Um, it's about Michael."

"Did he call you on his cell phone?"

"He called. I don't know if he was using a cell phone or not. And he's okay. Or he sounds like he's okay."

Grant's hopes lifted. "Tell me about the call."

"First, I've got to apologize," Randy said. "I

didn't mean to be nosy or anything. This just kinda happened. When your ex-wife showed up on skis and you two came up to the truck, I was messing around with the dogs. I guess I should have gotten out of the way and let you have your privacy, but I didn't. I kind of hung around and listened. So I knew about the kidnapping.''

"It's okay," Grant assured him.

"Are you sure?" Randy's voice quavered nervously. "I know it's not right to eavesdrop, but I couldn't help it."

In spite of Grant's anxiety about Michael, he took a moment to reassure the boy. "Sometimes, Randy, things happen for reasons we don't understand. I never would've told you about Michael's kidnapping. It's a terrible thing, too heavy a load. As it turns out, it's fortunate that you overheard."

"Really?"

"Absolutely. Because you can now help me. I want to know every detail about your phone call from Michael."

"He sounded tired. Otherwise, he seemed fine. Not scared or anything."

Grant looked toward Susan who hovered nervously beside him. To her, he said, "Michael is all right."

Her tear-filled eyes squeezed shut. "Thank God."

"Randy, hold on," Grant said. "I'm putting you on the speakerphone in my office. Michael's mother is here with me. We both need to hear what you have to say."

After a bit of telephone manipulation, Grant and Susan were both standing in the office, too tense to sit down.

Grant said, "Randy? Can you hear me?"

"Yeah."

"Go ahead. We're both listening."

"Hi, ma'am."

"It's Susan," she said. Though she tried to maintain her usual cheerfulness, there was an edge of hysteria in her unnaturally high-pitched voice. "Please call me Susan."

"Okay. Well, I was just telling Grant that I kinda overheard what you were talking about at the truck. So I knew Michael was kidnapped."

He paused, and Grant imagined the boy pushing an unruly hank of hair off his forehead.

"And I also knew you weren't supposed to tell the cops," Randy continued.

Grant held his breath. "Did you tell anyone else?"

"No way. I really wanted to tell my mom, but I was scared I'd mess stuff up for you."

"Good."

Randy Gaylor was a remarkable boy. Most teenagers would have been on the phone, blabbing about the kidnapping to all their buddies, but Randy had kept his own counsel.

"Just a little while ago," Randy said, "Michael telephoned me here at Mountain Rescue. I would've called you right away, but I couldn't because my mom was here, and I didn't want her to know."

"You did the right thing," Grant said. "What did Michael say?"

"He sounded really wiped out—you know, tired. The guys who took him gave him a shot in the butt that made him sleepy."

"They're drugging him," Susan whispered.

When Grant looked at her, he saw naked terror. Her complexion was ghostly white. Her arms clenched tightly beneath her breasts. She looked as if she might faint at any minute.

"Anyhow," Randy continued, "he said he was in a room with a bed, watching Saturn Patrol videotapes and waiting for his dad to pick him up."

"He hasn't been hurt?" Grant asked.

"The little dude is just sleepy. He sounded cool, just hanging out. I tried to get him to tell me where he was, but he doesn't know. He said there's a window in the room but he can't see anything but snow and trees."

"Did he mention a car accident?"

"No, nothing about an accident. But he told me he only woke up one time, and he saw Elephant Rock. I remembered that was where you take him fishing."

Grant knew the landmark well. It wasn't far from the Old Grange Road, where they'd found the disabled Jeep.

"We have to go there," Susan said. "We have to find him."

"What?" Randy asked.

She aimed her voice at the speaker. "Thank you, Randy. This means more to me than I can ever say."

"So you're not mad about me spying on you?"

"You've done everything right," Susan said.

"Was there anything else?" Grant asked.

"Nothing else. Like I said, he was tired. He said, 'Night, night, and don't let the bedbugs bite.'"

Hearing those innocent words tore a hole in Grant's heart. In a flash, he remembered all those nights when he'd tucked Michael into bed, smoothing the dark hair off his son's forehead and looking into his curious blue eyes. The sweet smell of childhood warmth assailed Grant's senses. He could almost hear Michael's voice, asking more and more questions in a blatant ploy to avoid the time when he was supposed to be sleeping. *Night, night, don't let the bedbugs bite.*

Apparently, a similar image had occurred to Susan and it overwhelmed her. She collapsed into a chair and sobbed silently into her hands.

Grant drew upon his last reserve of courage to keep from cracking. He wouldn't succumb to the pain and panic that twisted and churned in his gut. He needed to be strong, to do something to rescue his son.

In a steady voice, he spoke into the phone. "Randy, I have to ask you a big favor."

"Shoot."

This might be literally a matter of life and death. How could he put the weight of the responsibility on the shoulders of a fourteen-year-old boy? "If you don't feel like you can do it, that's all right. Just tell me."

"Okay."

"Don't say anything to anyone, not even your mom. We're going to pay off the kidnappers tomorrow at ten and get Michael back. We don't want to involve the authorities. We want to cooperate with the kidnappers."

"Sure," Randy said. "I understand."

"Do you think you can do that? Keep this secret until tomorrow at ten?"

"He's going to be okay, isn't he? Nothing bad will happen, will it?"

"Michael will be fine. These guys just want money. We'll give it to them, and this thing will be over."

Grant expressed more optimism than he truly felt. It seemed as if he was standing at the brink of a glacial abyss with hundred-mile-an-hour winds pushing him toward a hellish, icy plummet. His only defense was confidence—the belief that everything would turn out to be all right. "Can you do that, Randy?"

"Yeah."

"If Michael calls again, let me know. Call here at Pinedale. If I don't answer, leave a message on the machine."

"You got it."

Randy sounded better than when he first came on the phone. It must have been a relief for him to talk about Michael, and Grant spent a few more minutes reassuring the teenager and complimenting him on his intelligent behavior.

Without thinking, Grant had switched to the leadership tone he used in working with the volunteer Mountain Rescue teams. In the face of disaster, he had learned to remain calm. Battling the elements, his rescue team couldn't be hampered by their own fears and doubts.

There was always the chance that, at the end of their quest, they might find death. Yet they couldn't give up hope, couldn't stop believing there would be survivors.

"One more thing, Randy." Grant concentrated on the task at hand. "Jack wasn't there this afternoon. Is he back yet?"

"Nope. He's not due back here until tomorrow at the earliest. Maybe not until the next day."

Damn. Another complication. Grant had hoped Jack would be able to fly them into Denver and back. It seemed that each time he tried to grab hold of the reins, they slipped from his grasp.

"My mom's going to be back," Randy said helpfully. "She's off running errands before the blizzard hits, but she said she had to make a call to California before we go home at seven."

"Thanks for letting me know." Jack's absence would make it harder to hitch a plane ride into town, but Grant wouldn't give up. He couldn't. Michael needed him. Into the phone he said, "Okay, Randy. Hang in there, buddy."

"Good luck, Grant."

Grant disconnected the call and looked over at Susan, who was still weeping soundlessly, helplessly. How the hell could he comfort this woman who despised him? How could he ease her pain? It appeared as if he would have to be strong enough for both of them, but he wasn't feeling very heroic. Fear rose like bile in his throat. His stomach tightened into a hard knot.

"I'll be right back," he said to her.

He went into the small bathroom adjoining the office and closed the door. Bracing his hands on the sink, he breathed deeply. His gaze ricocheted off the sterile walls of the small cubicle, avoiding his reflection in the mirror, since it might show his terror and undermine his resolve. He had to get Michael back. If he failed...

He gagged. Bending over, Grant vomited into the toilet.

AFTER HE gained his composure, Grant joined Susan in the lobby. A frightening stillness had come over her.

"Are you hungry?" he asked.

"Are you?"

He'd just puked up his guts. Now was not the time to think about food. "No."

"I'm so confused, Grant. One part of me wants to get the money and wait, and trust that the kidnappers will release Michael. Another part wants to track them down."

"I know." He felt the same way.

"Where's Elephant Rock?"

"It's just off the main road. On the route we took when we went to O'Dell's place."

"Could they be hiding Michael there?"

"Maybe." Apparently Michael had awakened and had seen the rock. "But it's possible that Michael only saw the rock as they drove past in the car. Or it might be right outside where he's being kept."

"At least we know they're still in this area," she said. "Michael must have used the cell phone, and it doesn't have a strong signal. I wish I knew the exact range, but the reception seems to vary, depending upon weather and the position in the mountains."

"Let's assume they're somewhere in the Rampart River Valley. Which means they're not more than ten miles away."

Unfortunately, a ten-mile radius included unlimited possibilities. Within ten miles, there were mountains, hills, valleys, caves, the town of Rampart and the construction site of Sven Dahlberg's condominiums. Even if they notified the state patrol, a controlled, surreptitious search was virtually impossible.

Still, he asked, "Should we notify the authorities?"

"How could they help?"

"An APB on O'Dell's truck. They could do a door-to-door search, but they can't enter a cabin without a warrant."

"No." Her answer was quick and decisive. "I won't take that risk."

"What about our own search? Should we try to find him?"

She exhaled heavily. Her flood of tears seemed to have washed away some of the tension, eroding her fear. In spite of the puffiness around her eyes, she looked tougher and more determined.

"Okay, Grant. We'll search. But we've got to keep an eye on the clock. What about the plane? Is that taken care of?"

"Don't worry about it."

"Are you sure? If we're driving, we should get under way."

"I'll take care of the transportation."

As he rose from the chair in the lobby, Grant experienced a jolt of adrenaline that energized his limbs. Working with mountain rescues had prepared him for this task. He was accustomed to pushing himself to the limit, overcoming the odds. "Let me put the dogs away and feed them. Then we'll be on our way to Elephant Rock."

"I'll come with you. I want to see the mutts."

Outside, he called to Maud, Mabel and Snuffy, who were still hanging around at the far end of the hotel by the indoor parking garage. Grant led his little troop around the west end of the hotel to the enclosure, while Susan brought up the rear.

Softly she chatted with Snuffy about what the dog had been digging for, and she lavished compliments on all three animals, telling them how beautiful and smart they were.

His dogs adored her. Even when she ceased to be

the primary supplier of their twice-daily meals, they loved to get attention from Susan.

As always, he was impressed by how easily she related to both man and beast. Everybody loved Susan. Instinctively, she knew the right things to say. When she'd exploded in the hotel after the kidnapper's phone call, telling Grant that he'd made her life a living hell, it was only the fourth or fifth time he'd heard her lose control.

My God, had he hurt her so badly? He'd been so wrapped up in his own bereavement after the fire that he hadn't been able to look beyond himself. Ignoring her and Michael had been unintentional, but she was right—one-hundred-percent right. He'd been a monster to live with, and it had taken him months after she and Michael were gone to come to his senses.

Even now, when he thought he'd gotten past his obsession, he had a hard time accepting the fire and Rachel's death. At Doc Evanston's house, when Donny had accused him of being responsible for his sister's death, Grant had experienced a painful shock.

"Oh, my," Susan remarked when she beheld the dogs' enclosure. "You did a great job with this."

"Nothing's too good for my dogs."

"I guess not. This looks like a penthouse suite for canines."

Chain-link fence marked off a huge area at the far-west end of the hotel. The fence started only a few feet back from the steep drop-off that led down to the wild, rushing Rampart River, a waterway that was too wide and fast to ever freeze over completely, not even in the depths of winter.

The roar of the river was an integral part of Pinedale's charm, a constant reminder that the hotel wasn't in some Denver suburb. The rear of the hotel bordered on the embankment at the river's edge. Guests in the back rooms could look out on an incredible display of nature.

In the dogs' compound, three lamps, like streetlights, shed illumination on their enclosure. The floor was part concrete, part snowpack and part straw. There were three large doghouses with plastic flaps covering the doors. Clean straw filled the interiors. There was also a good-size shed, where Grant kept his dogsled. All these outbuildings were insulated.

When they approached, the entire dog pack was in the yard, near the gate, and Grant couldn't help smiling as he beheld the sea of wagging tails and thick, lustrous coats.

Including Mabel and Maud, there were six Siberian husky sled dogs. Their markings varied in color from black to silver to sable, and they all had the white-tipped tail of purebreds. The unquestioned lead dog, Amble, strutted among the others. Duke, the youngest, always had a confused expression in his amber, almond-shaped eyes. The two bigger, heavier malamutes—a little standoffish—were wheel dogs on the sled. And Pyrite, a tracker like Snuffy, was another golden retriever.

As he filled their bowls with food and water, Susan greeted the sled dogs, paying special attention to Pyrite, her favorite. She'd named him as a puppy, when he'd stolen a fresh-made blueberry pie from the kitchen, staining his nose purple. He'd bounded up to greet her with the pie pan in his mouth. Instead of being angry, Susan had laughed and said, ''This gold dog is such a fool, he doesn't know when he's done something wrong. Fool's gold. Let's call him Pyrite.''

Her reunion with Pyrite was enthusiastic, and Grant was glad that she had this brief respite. From experience, he knew that the dogs were good companions. They were always loyal and affectionate, even when everything else was going straight to hell.

As she played with them, Susan laughed, and the sound was more beautiful than a violin concerto played on a Stradivarius. It had been a long time since he'd heard the sound of her amusement.

"I've got a couple of things to do before we leave," he told her. "You stay here, and I'll pull the truck around to this end."

"I'll be here with the dogs. I didn't realize how much I've missed these crazy mutts."

When she looked up, her cheeks were pink. Her lips parted in a familiar grin that stirred his blood. He still thought she was the most beautiful woman on earth. "I'll be right back."

Quickly he gathered up a few necessary items from the hotel and returned with the truck to the dog enclosure. After locking up, he and Susan set out for Elephant Rock. It wasn't far, about a fifteen-minute drive.

At the main highway, his headlights slashed through the gathering dusk. The day skiers had left earlier, and the road was sparsely traveled. Had Doc Evanston returned to his home? He might be there right now, getting an earful from Donny and wondering why Grant and Susan Richardson had paid a call. Or Doc might know exactly why they had come to his house. He might be deriving some satisfaction from their panic.

Though it was hard to believe that this kind, elderly gentleman could be involved in a kidnapping, Grant remembered Doc's pain when Rachel died. His beautiful daughter had been taken from him. As far as he knew, Rachel had been faultless. A terrific athlete. Bright. Vivacious. "She was perfect," he mused.

"Who?"

He hadn't planned to mention the fire again, but he and Susan needed to talk about possible motives. "Rachel," he said. "I was thinking about the possibility of Doc or Donny hiring the kidnappers. Then I thought about Doc's sorrow. It seems especially tragic because she was so incredible."

"But not perfect," Susan said.

"What do you mean?"

"Don't you remember? She and Charley were having some problems. A couple of times, I thought she was downright mean to him. She'd flirt with other men, right in his face, then she'd turn around and tell me that Charley was too jealous."

"Did he have reason to be?"

"She was headstrong," Susan remembered, "and men adored her. I always let Rachel talk to the contractors and suppliers because she could charm the pants off them."

"Literally?"

"I don't know if she was unfaithful, but she loved attention from men. Also, she and Charley were in disagreement about having a baby. He wanted one. She didn't."

Grant recalled his own conversations with Charley Beacham. He'd been eight years older than Rachel when they married, and he'd talked about wanting her to grow up. He'd thought the renovation of Pinedale would help her to settle down. Instead, it had killed her.

"What's in the backpack?" Susan asked.

"Mountain-rescue supplies," he said. "You know I always keep a pack ready."

She dug through it, enumerating objects as she found them. "First-aid kit. Swiss Army knife. Extra gloves. Extra cap. Aha! This is what I was looking for. Granola."

"I thought you weren't hungry."

"Changed my mind."

"Good," he said. "On a rescue, you have to keep up your strength. Drink plenty of water. Eat when necessary."

"Is that what we're doing?" she asked. "Going on a rescue?"

He sure as hell hoped they could find and rescue Michael. "Could be."

She chewed a mouthful of crunchy granola. "This is awful."

"Store-bought," he said. "It's nowhere near as good as the granola you used to make for me."

"That's because I happen to be a master chef."

"And a damn good cook."

They exchanged a smile. This light teasing was familiar from the good years of their marriage.

"My cooking," she said. "That was the only reason you married me, wasn't it?"

"You bet," he kidded. "I managed to ignore the fact that you were the prettiest woman I'd ever seen. Hey, I even disregarded your smarts, your sense of humor and the way you could blow in my ear and make me crazy. All I was looking for was a wench who could rustle up a hearty meal."

"Thought so."

Susan felt immeasurably better. Though she had

hated herself for bursting into tears, she'd been cleansed by the torrent of her emotion. And Randy's phone call had given her reason to hope. Though she didn't like the fact that Michael was being drugged to keep him quiet, it was a relief to know he wasn't being terrorized. The best thing, actually, was for him to sleep through the entire ordeal. And if they could rescue him tonight, right now...

After Grant had pulled off the main road and driven half a mile, she recognized Elephant Rock, a towering, snowcapped oblong of granite, with a single crevice at one end that marked the elephant's trunk. She'd been here with Grant when he worked with the rescue team on rock climbing. "Where did you take Michael fishing around here?"

"We were practicing with fly casting and I let him wade in Skunk Creek."

A pleasant picture formed in her mind. She thought of a sunny day. Grant and Michael—her two men— would be tromping along the skinny creek with their poles and gear. Now, the landscape was dark, wintry and foreboding.

He parked and they both scanned the area.

"Michael is in a room with a television set and a window," she said. "That rules out caves and abandoned shacks."

"I wish I knew who else lived along this road. We seem to keep coming back here."

"We could ask Addie, the postmistress."

"Excellent idea. We'll call her."

"I don't suppose this is near anything obvious, like Sven Dahlberg's condos."

"They're in the opposite direction." Grant pointed.

"I see a cabin over there, but it doesn't look like there are any lights on."

She squinted through the hazy darkness. It was a quarter past six, and the early-winter dusk had settled. Overhead, the North Star shone brightly through the mist that had settled like a cloud on the high country. Though a blizzard might hit tomorrow, the night promised to be fairly clear.

The outline of a cabin was visible in the direction he'd indicated. It stood beside a copse of ponderosa pine on a plateau above a field of soft white snow. As she stared, Susan thought she detected a faint bluish glow coming from one room. "A television," she said.

"What?"

"Don't you see it, Grant? In the far left corner, there's a sort of soft, bluish glow, like the light from a television."

"And Michel was watching videos."

Her heart beat fast to think that her son might be so near. "Drive on ahead," she said. "The kidnappers might be watching the road."

He pulled around a bend and parked at the side of the road about a mile away from the plateau and the cabin. The headlights went dead and night surrounded them.

She looked to Grant to take charge and was willing to defer to his judgment. This was his territory, and he would know exactly what to do.

"There's got to be a turnoff and a driveway that leads up to the cabin," he said. "But it's smarter if we don't alert them to our presence. Our best approach is to climb over those rocks behind the cabin and make a descent from there. They won't be expecting anyone to come from the rear.''

''The long way around.'' And the most precipitous. Susan had learned the basics of rock climbing when she and Grant were together, but she'd been born and raised in the city. She'd never been totally comfortable with heights. ''Do you think Michael is there?''

''I don't know, but I want to take a look around.''

Were they chasing snowflakes in the wind? She didn't know, but she did know they had to check out every possibility. ''We have to try,'' she stated with conviction.

''Good.''

She glanced at her wristwatch. ''If we're going to make the drive all the way to Denver and back, we need to leave by seven o'clock. That's only forty-five minutes from now.''

''Let me worry about getting us back and forth to Denver.'' He was already sorting through his emergency backpack and another duffel bag full of equipment. ''I'll take my snowshoes. Your cross-country skis are still in the back of the truck.''

''What if they're armed?''

He held up a semiautomatic pistol. ''So are we.''

The sheen of moonlight against gunmetal reminded her that they weren't on an average search-and-rescue patrol, helping a stranded skier climb out of a snowbank. ''Do you think—''

''Yes,'' he said. ''Back at O'Dell's cabin, when I went charging up the stairs thinking the kidnappers might be there, I wished for a gun.''

''We don't want to get into a shoot-out, Grant. They could hurt Michael.''

''It won't come to that.''

"It can't," she insisted. "Don't make me give you the don't-be-a-hero speech again."

"This is only reconnaissance. Our goal is to determine if the kidnappers and Michael are at this cabin. Then we'll decide if we need the gun or not."

Uneasily, she agreed.

The bitter cold sliced through her as she fastened the bindings on her Nordic skis. Wisps of moisture swirled around her. The soft moonlight tinted the landscape an unearthly blue. And the night was silent—heavily, portentously still—and full of secrets.

"No loud talking," he reminded her. "Voices carry in this kind of darkness."

Like echoes of disaster. She wasn't sure if they were doing the right thing by approaching the cabin. But how could she hold back? "I'm right behind you."

They traversed a meadow of snow. The thought of finding Michael had given her renewed vigor, and she barely felt her bruises as she followed Grant. At the forest's edge, he located a trail through the pines and conifers. Only an expert mountaineer, like Grant, would have noticed the slight parting in the trees and the narrow path worn by deer and elk.

Was Michael there? She hardly dared to hope, but she'd seen the blue light that had to come from a television. And wasn't it suspicious that the rest of the cabin was dark?

Ahead of her, jogging heavily in his waffle-bottomed snowshoes, Grant halted and motioned for her to come up close beside him.

"Take off the skis," he said. His voice was as quiet as the wind in the pines. "We need to climb over these rocks. Then we'll be directly behind the cabin."

"Are you sure?"

He nodded, and she had no doubt that he knew exactly where he was. His internal compass was more accurate than a global-positioning satellite receiver.

Surefooted, without his snowshoes, he climbed ahead of her on the slippery, snow-covered rocks and held out his hand. It wasn't a difficult ascent, requiring pitons and ropes, but she needed his help, especially in the dark, since she couldn't see the crevices to brace her feet and her gloved hands.

He pulled her up beside him on a ledge and whispered, "It's only about twenty feet higher."

Swiftly he moved ahead, helped her, then climbed higher until they were at the crest of the rocks, lying flat in the snow and peering down at the cabin.

It seemed deserted. There were no tracks in the drifts of snow. All the curtains were drawn, and there was only a faint blue glow from the corner room.

Grant placed the gun in her hand. "I'm going down to take a look. If you see anyone, fire a warning shot."

"You're just going to look. Right?"

"I'll be right back."

Stealthy as a shadow, he glided down from their perch. From somewhere in the distance, she heard the howl of a coyote, and the plaintive sound shivered through her.

She removed her glove and held the gun in her hand. Once or twice, she'd taken target practice with the Rampart locals, but Susan didn't really know how to use a gun. Not being a hunter, she wasn't capable of more than vaguely aiming and pulling a trigger.

As Grant crept closer to the cabin, she had an urge to call him back. If they caught him, what would happen? She remembered the shorter kidnapper's harsh treatment of her and the coldness she'd seen in his eyes.

Grant was at the window, peering inside. As her tension heightened, he circled the cabin, heading from one window to the next. When he came around to the far side, he waved with both arms. "False alarm. It's a grow light for plants. Nobody's here."

She blinked away her fears. "Are you sure?"

"Nobody but you and me and the moonlight."

In a few minutes, he was back beside her. "We'll climb down from here, Susan. It's easier, and we can take the road back to the car. I'll get the skis and snowshoes."

Swallowing her disappointment, she nodded. This had seemed so right, so close. "I thought we were on the right track."

"This wasn't a dead loss."

"No?"

"In case you hadn't noticed, we're working together. Like a team."

And it felt so right. "Once upon a time, we were a really good team."

"Damn good," he said.

"Well, partner," she said. "We'd better hit the road if we're going to make it to Denver."

"It's not going to take that long."

"What are you talking about? It's five hours there and five hours back."

He shrugged. "Not if we steal an airplane."

Chapter Six

It was only half past seven, but it seemed much later. This had to be the longest day of Susan's life.

In the shadows on the road near Slade's Adventures, Grant glided the truck to a silent stop, and they sat, waiting and listening.

"All right," he said. "I think it's safe."

"Is it really? Is this plan of yours truly safe?"

"Have you got a better idea?"

He opened his door and grabbed the backpack that rested on the seat between them—the backpack containing the handgun. "Grant, is that necessary? Do you need the gun?"

He flashed a glistening white smile. "Let me tell you a little something about being a hero. The trick is to survive. Until this is over, I'm armed."

She didn't like the idea, but conceded.

When she closed the passenger-side door, the metallic clunk seemed to resound as loudly as an explosion of TNT. Every noise was magnified in the silent night. As they hiked toward the office, her boots crunched on the crusted roadside snow. Surely someone would hear. Surely someone would stop them.

"I can't believe we're doing this," she muttered.

"There's not much choice," Grant said. "Jack's not around to give us a lift into Denver."

"We could call around to other charter services," she suggested. They were quite a distance from Aspen and Vail, but there were smaller airfields. "What about that, Grant?"

"In the first place, they'd have to follow FAA regs, file a flight plan and all the rest. We'd have to get Jill Gaylor down here to okay the landing which means we'd have to tell her what's going on."

"I trust Jill."

"So do I. She's a good person. But people are going to ask questions about why we were flying off in the middle of the night."

"That's true."

"Plus we've got some bad weather coming in. Most pilots won't take a charter unless it's an emergency. Do you want to tell them about the emergency?"

"No," she said.

He flashed a smile. "Besides, Sven Dahlberg owes me a favor."

"If we get caught—"

"We won't get caught," he said confidently. "Sven isn't going to miss his Cessna. Right now, he's probably curled up in front of a fireplace sharing a hot buttered rum with his slinky little secretary, Melanie."

She eyed Grant suspiciously. Was the theft of an airplane another example of his need for dramatic heroics? She liked being partners with him, but hijacking seemed more like reckless stupidity than sensible bravery. As far as she knew, Grant didn't even know how to fly.

She smiled to herself. Susan had a couple of tricks up her sleeve on that count.

At the front door of Slade's Adventures, Grant used his key—issued in case of a Mountain Rescue emergency. Inside, he turned on his flashlight. "Slade keeps extra keys for the planes that hangar here. They're in his desk."

Inside Jack Slade's private office, Grant went to the desk and tugged on the top-left drawer. "Damn, it's locked."

"That shouldn't be a problem," she said. "What's a little more breaking and entering?"

"I'm not enjoying this," he replied as he set to work on the lock with his pocketknife. "But, I'll tell you one thing for sure, I don't feel bad about stealing from Sven Dahlberg. He's a world-class jerk and he might be..." His voice trailed off.

"Dahlberg might be...what?" she demanded.

Grant knelt so he would be at eye level with the desk lock, and she crouched down beside him, peering through the pale moonlight from the windows, watching his expression carefully.

"Here, Susan. Hold the flashlight on the lock so I can see."

Instead, she aimed the beam directly on him like a miniature spotlight. "Tell me about Sven Dahlberg."

He adjusted the light so it focused on the desk lock. "Sven might be involved in the kidnapping. Like I said before, he wants Pinedale and he tried to buy me out."

"I don't get the connection. What does a condo developer who wants your land have to do with our son?"

"Ever since Sven started work up here, about a

year ago, he's been riding my butt. He's created problems with the town council on my permits and paid off inspectors to say I didn't meet code on my electric and plumbing."

Susan couldn't imagine how an outsider like Sven could turn the town council against Grant. The people of Rampart protected their own, and her ex-husband had done a lot of good in this area. Before she and Grant had settled here, the local volunteer rescue team had been little more than a couple of guys who sometimes did some rock climbing. With Grant's help, the rescue unit had been trained effectively.

Of course, some of the people in Rampart still blamed Grant for the fire and Rachel's death. After the tragedy, they'd needed someone to hate, and they had turned on Grant. Some said he was responsible because he'd been working everybody too hard. Others claimed that Pinedale, itself, was cursed, and Grant never should have tried to open the place.

But Susan had seen their grief and anger fade. When she'd left Grant, several townspeople had expressed their heartfelt sadness at the breakup of their marriage. They'd offered consolation, not blame.

Again she looked at Grant, who was concentrating hard on the lock, trying not to scar the wooden desk. Though they were no longer married, he was still a good man, an admirable human being. "How could this Sven person have turned the town council against you?"

"The fire."

"I can't believe people are still holding a grudge."

"Sven kept bringing it up, picking at the old sadness, reopening the wound and pouring salt into it. He reminded people that I'm not a safe person to be around. At his instigation, the Rampart Council organized the Rachel Evanston Beacham Memorial Fund for college scholarships.''

"Still, you have a lot of friends here.''

"I don't know about that.''

"Don't give me that 'aw, shucks' attitude.'' Though Grant loved to play the hero, he was the last person to accept accolades. She continued, ''I know that you led the rescue for those four cross-country skiers who were stranded. You saved their lives. And there were the two seven-year-old boys who got lost when they went hiking. Also, if I'm not mistaken, the U.S. Air Force contacted you to help find that A-10 plane that went missing.''

"So?''

"People respect you. How could Sven change that?''

"*Some* people respect me,'' he said. ''As you pointed out, I'm not the easiest person to be around. I want my contract jobs done right, and I don't tolerate sloppy work.''

Not an endearing trait. ''It isn't much fun to work for a perfectionist.''

"I've had a hell of a time getting employees and keeping them. That's why I've had to hire morons like O'Dell.''

"You're still not explaining why Sven would stoop to kidnapping.''

"He's greedy and stubborn. He'll go to any lengths to get what he wants.''

"Even kidnapping?''

"I'm thinking of the money,'' he said. ''Four hundred and fifty thou is enough to break me during the first year of operations. If I go broke, I won't have any choice but to sell, and Sven wants Pinedale."

He popped open the drawer. Within, he found a metal box, similar to those used by fishermen to carry their flies. Inside the box were various keys, all neatly tagged. He held up a small metal ring with four keys. It was marked "Dahlberg, Cessna."

"Success," Grant said.

"Swell," Susan said. "Now we only have a few tiny obstacles. Like taking off on a dark field. Flying in bad weather. Oh, yes, and your inexperience. Tell me again, Grant, how many times have you piloted a small plane?"

"Jack Slade has been giving me some instruction. Sometimes he has to fly a plane back to its original destination, and he takes me along. He's shown me how it works. Once, he let me land."

"I see. And how many times have you flown solo?"

"Never," Grant admitted.

"Well, I have." She snatched the keys from his hand and picked her way through the dimly lit office toward the exit.

"What do you mean, Susan? You've soloed?"

"Twenty-three hours' solo time."

She savored this moment of triumph. For once, the heroic Grant Richardson would be relegated to the copilot's seat while she took over as captain. Susan stepped out into the night and headed toward the hangar.

He was right beside her. "When did you learn how to fly?"

"We've been separated for two years, Grant. I

haven't spent every minute of that time in the restaurant, whipping up the best pesto in Denver.''

''Your little brother is a pilot,'' he remembered.

''He took me up a couple of times. I enjoyed it and started taking lessons on my own.'' At the door to the hangar, she faced him. ''Why do you think I even agreed to consider this scheme? Because I trusted your ability as a pilot?''

''Because of Michael?''

''It wouldn't do our son any good for both of his parents to be killed in a plane crash.'' She faced him. ''And yes, I'm doing this for Michael.''

In less compelling circumstances, she never would have considered taking off at night in threatening weather. The approach on the Rampart landing strip was only half a mile, marked by trees at one end and the town on the other. The tarmac was poorly cleared, but she assumed that since Sven often took off and landed in snow, he had the correct gear and tires for rough landings.

Inside the hangar, she and Grant went to work, doing a quick preflight inspection of the Cessna. ''We'll get more fuel in Denver,'' she said. ''Otherwise, it looks good. I'm familiar with these instruments. If I can manage the takeoff, we should be okay.''

''Maybe we ought to drive,'' Grant said.

''Having second thoughts?'' she teased. ''You just can't stand not being in control. Don't you think I can do it?''

''I trust you, Susan. I trust you with my life.''

His comment pleased her, and she smiled up into his brilliant blue eyes. Within her breast, she felt a flicker of the old passion they once had shared. ''Open the hangar door.''

HE HADN'T COUNTED ON the airplane. He peered through the trees, watching Susan and Grant as they stirred the cobalt shadows of the January night, and he cursed this oversight. His plan was for them to be completely occupied with the drive to Denver and back. He didn't want them to stay here in the valley, sniffing around.

It was a damn good thing that he'd picked up their trail and followed. Of course, he'd had to go out anyway. O'Dell's rattletrap truck was almost out of gas, and he didn't want to take any chances on running dry during his getaway.

Though he'd taken a risk by filling up at the gas station, he wasn't planning to hang around. Rampart was history. When his revenge on Grant was complete and Susan was dead, he would have no more use for the little mountain town that had once felt like the most beautiful place on earth.

Damn Grant Richardson for thinking of the airplane! Like a cat, he always landed on his feet.

Not anymore. Silently, he slid back into the trees.

Maybe Sven would like to know what was going on with his airplane.

AFTER SHE'D TAXIED ONTO the runway, Grant closed the hangar doors and took his position in the copilot's seat beside her. It didn't seem right to be riding shotgun. Though he trusted Susan, he didn't like to be second-in-command.

As she expertly directed the Cessna to the end of the runway and lined up for takeoff, he offered information. "I know how to turn on the runway lights from the plane."

"Good. Go ahead."

"It's a risk. Somebody might notice."

"Flying blind is more dangerous."

Grant adjusted the radio frequency and punched in the signal. Automatically, lights on either side of the runway came to life. "They're on a timer," he said. "They'll go off in fifteen minutes."

She nodded. "A lot of these unmanned runways have this system."

He settled back in the copilot's seat. They were both wearing headsets, conversing through the intercom microphones over the whir of the small plane's propellers. "Susan, is there something else I can do?"

"You can pray."

Overhead, he could still see stars. The wispy clouds had not completely consumed the night. The wind sock atop Slade's Adventures barely floated in the wind. They were in the calm before the blizzard. He gritted his teeth as she turned on the Cessna's running lights.

"Ready?" she asked.

"Do it."

He'd meant what he said before. He trusted her. In spite of everything—the acrimony of their divorce and their constant sniping—he believed in her. But now Susan was almost a stranger to him. He hadn't known she could fly a plane. He was ignorant of so many things about her life. She'd said that she was keeping the accounts for her father's restaurants, but when she'd been working with Grant on Pinedale, Susan had disdained anything that had to do with numbers.

Her life without him was so completely different. She was a single mother and a competent career woman, who could manage to put her hands on four hundred and fifty thousand dollars with only a few hours' notice. Somehow, she seemed more competent than when they'd been together.

This beautiful stranger came from a world he knew little about. Finding out about her suddenly seemed very important to him. She was the mother of his son. They'd shared so much.

"Three, two, one," she said. "Takeoff."

Grant forced himself to keep his eyes open. If they were going to meet death on this short runway, he wanted to face the end head-on.

But Susan easily made the liftoff, soaring up over the trees into the night. They climbed above the clouds into black velvet skies filled with stars.

"I'll have to navigate by instrument," she said. "We can't see any landmarks through the clouds."

"Lucky for us that Sven has maps."

"And an air-to-ground phone," she added. "When we get close to Denver, I'll call my brother and arrange for fueling at the Tech Center Airport."

"How long will the flight take?"

"It's about one hundred and thirteen air miles. That should take an hour, maybe fifteen minutes longer, depending on head winds and air traffic." She stared straight ahead. "As you know, I'm not very good about being punctual."

"Being late isn't exactly an endearing habit, Susan."

"Nor is clock watching."

He gazed at her fine-boned profile. The headset seemed big and cumbersome on her. Her hands on the yoke were small and delicate. A remarkable woman. He wanted to know everything about her, to see how she'd changed and how she was the same. "Let's not bicker."

"We don't have much else left," she said. "We're divorced, Grant. We share a common interest in Michael, but that's where our relationship stops."

"It doesn't have to end there."

She turned toward him. "I want to make this perfectly clear. Things can never be the way they once were."

"We were good together."

"Yes," she said. "We were wonderful. But that was the past. I can't go through the pain of breaking up. Never again."

Stubbornly he reminded, "We agreed to act as partners."

"Only when it comes to our son."

Though he wanted to tell her that he was different, that he'd gotten over his obsession, now wasn't the time. "Fine." He nodded brusquely.

There were more important things to think about. There was Michael.

Grant wasn't a praying kind of man. He believed in using his own resources and not whining to anybody for help. Yet, as they streaked through the heavens, above his beloved Rocky Mountains, he closed his eyes and silently offered up a heartfelt, silent wish for a happy ending. He beseeched the universe to help his son.

Randy Gaylor had said that Michael didn't seem scared, just sleepy. Grant prayed that his son wouldn't wake up until he was safe in the loving arms of his father and mother.

Together, they would hold him. And Susan might see past her hurt to know that he still cared for her.

THEY'D MADE GOOD TIME on the flight. Susan had contacted her brother and arranged to refuel the Cessna. She'd also borrowed his car.

It was nine-thirty, more than twelve hours until they needed to pay off the kidnappers. At the south Denver restaurant she managed, Susan parked in the back. She turned off the ignition, but her hand lingered on the door handle. She didn't want to leave the car, didn't want to walk inside and face the task that lay before her.

"Scared?" Grant asked.

"Apprehensive."

Her plan was to work through Mama. Carolyn Falcone was less volatile and could offer the best advice for dealing with Susan's father. Mama was wise, sensitive and clever. She would know what to do, how to handle Daddy.

Yet Susan would almost rather face her father's explosive temper than see renewed pain in her mother's careworn face.

Grant touched her arm. "A shrink would say it's good to talk about your feelings."

She sighed. "When I left you, I felt something like this. Apprehensive. Of course, Michael was with me then, asleep in his car seat. I'd loaded the van, driven down from Rampart, and I sat outside this restaurant, maybe in this very space, gathering my courage to break the news to Mama."

Her marriage had failed. She'd memorized a list of good, sensible reasons for why she must leave Grant. She needed to do what was right for herself, to get on with her life. It wasn't the end of the world. Change could be a good thing.

The words had echoed hollow as a dirge. The only truth was failure.

When she'd talked to Mama about her separation, Susan had tried to be positive, but the undisguised sadness in her mother's expression had been her undoing. Slowly, Mama had taken both her hands. Carolyn's motions had been heavy, as if she'd been lifting the weight of the world, and she'd said two words, "I'm sorry."

Susan's forced hopes had crumbled. She was sorry, too. Sorry for herself, for Michael, for Grant. She'd collapsed in her mother's arms and wept. It had felt as though she'd cried for hours. Even after her tears had run dry, convulsive sobs had shaken her body like dry heaves.

Leaving Grant, losing his love, was the greatest tragedy she had ever endured. Until now.

She pushed open the door of her brother's car. "Let's go."

Grant met her at the front of the car. "Do you want me to do the talking?"

"I wish you could." It would have felt so much safer to hide behind Grant, to allow him to handle this terrible negotiation. "This is my family. I have to face them."

In the restaurant's kitchen, Susan spied the slim, graceful figure of Carolyn Falcone. She was dressed in chef's white. Her long brown hair, liberally streaked with gray, was tucked inside a drooping chef's hat. She was leaning over a stainless-steel counter, studying the next day's menu.

"Mama."

When Carolyn looked up and saw her daughter, accompanied by her ex-husband, her hazel eyes brightened in a flash of hope. Mama had never given up on the possibility of a reconciliation. Her gentle alto voice lilted, "Susan and Grant. You've come to tell me something important."

"Not good news," Susan said.

Quickly, Carolyn's energy faded. Worry lines etched a frown around her mouth. "Both of you, come with me to the office."

They followed her into a small office with a desk, several locked files and a large, old-fashioned safe. It was the office Susan used when managing this restaurant. On the desktop was a photograph of Michael and a plaster cast of his small handprint that he'd made in preschool. In the corner was a toy box, filled with his favorite things because she often brought him to work with her. It felt strange to be ushered inside.

Carolyn closed the door behind them. She hugged Grant. "It's good to see you, young man."

"And you, Carolyn."

"You were always my favorite son-in-law."

"I was your only son-in-law," he said.

"True." Carolyn heaved a sigh. "I'd think with four children over the age of twenty that they should all be married and giving me lots of grandchildren. That's my dream, Grant."

His smile was sincere. "You deserve to have your dreams fulfilled."

Carolyn stepped away from him and turned toward her daughter. "What's wrong, Susan?"

"I need for you to talk to Daddy." Her mouth was so dry that when she swallowed, she was gulping air. "I need some money. A lot of money, but I can't tell him why."

Carolyn glanced back and forth between them. "Is this for Pinedale?"

"No," Grant said.

Leaning against the edge of the desk, Carolyn folded her arms beneath her breasts and looked at Susan. "How much?"

"Four hundred and fifty thousand. In cash. Tonight."

Her mother blinked at the amount but said nothing.

"Mama, before I tell you anything else, you've got to promise that you'll do as I say. Even if it seems imprudent."

Carolyn nodded. "All right."

"You can't tell Daddy why we need this money. I'm afraid of what he might do."

"I won't lie to him, Susan. No good ever came from a lie. And I have always, always told your father the truth."

Though Susan agreed with her mother's high moral standards, this was different. If it took lying to save Michael, Susan would shout falsehoods from the peak of Mount Evans. "Promise you won't tell him."

"What is it?"

There was no gentle way to break the news. "Michael's been kidnapped."

Carolyn's lower lip trembled. Her hands freed themselves and gestured helplessly before clasping together beneath her chin, unconsciously assuming an attitude of prayer. "My God."

When she looked up, fear had paralyzed her features. Her eyes were guarded. "You need the money for ransom."

"We're supposed to pay the money tomorrow morning at ten o'clock. If we don't inform the police or the FBI, the kidnappers will return Michael unharmed.''

Carolyn looked at Grant. ''Do you agree with this?''

''I trust Susan's decision to pay them.''

Susan caught hold of her mother's clenched hands and squeezed tightly. ''We have to do what the kidnappers say. If we don't, they could hurt Michael. Do you understand?''

''But what makes you think they'll do as they promised?''

''Please, do it my way. Please,'' she begged. ''You can't tell Daddy until this is over. He'd go crazy.''

''Oh, you're right about that.'' Carolyn winced. ''If he knew, he'd be calling his friends in the police department, the state patrol, the governor.''

''We have to get the money from him without saying what it's for.'' As she spoke, Susan realized the futility of this task. Nobody told her father what to do. Nobody could stand up to his domineering will. ''But how?''

Carolyn shook her head. ''We can't ask your father for four hundred and fifty thousand dollars out of the clear blue sky. Not without a reason.''

Susan's fragile hopes shattered like crystal against concrete. How else could they get the ransom? Mentally she calculated how much money would be in the safe at this restaurant and the others. Even if they hadn't made the regular daily deposits yet, it wouldn't be anywhere near enough. ''Mama, how can we tell him?''

Carolyn glanced at her wristwatch. ''Your father is going to be here any minute.''

''Why?''

"Your brother called and said you and Grant were coming." She looked down at her hands. "I thought you'd have good news, and I wanted Pete to be here."

Quickly, Susan blurted out several false scenarios, ranging from needing money to remarry Grant to overdue tax bills.

Carolyn rejected each one with variations on the same answer. "He's my husband. I won't lie to him."

When Pete Falcone swaggered through the door, Susan regarded him with trepidation. Her handsome, vigorous father held the fate of Michael in his strong hands. He would want to take charge, and she didn't trust him.

Grant was the first to make a move. He approached Pete with his hand outstretched. "It's good to see you, sir."

Her father's thick, white head of hair ducked down as he considered the protocol for dealing with an ex-son-in-law, then he accepted Grant's handshake. "I always liked you, kid. How's your hotel?"

"Opening next week. Fully booked."

"And the restaurant?"

"I've already booked two wedding receptions."

"Catering?"

"I'm using the local caterer."

"Bush-league," Pete said with a dismissive sneer. "When you want a classy wedding, you come to me. I can work something out."

Carolyn stepped forward. Her voice quivered as she said, "Isn't this wonderful, Pete! Susan and Grant are considering a reconciliation."

Aghast, Susan stared at her mother. Carolyn had told a lie.

"Yes," Carolyn said. Her discomfort was obvious.

"They flew down here tonight because they wanted us to be the first to know."

Pete clapped Grant on the shoulder. "I always knew you were a stand-up guy. You come with me. We'll open a bottle of wine and talk about your hotel. Are you going to make some good profit?"

"I hope so."

"I've been thinking about hotels myself. I'm losing money hand over fist with these restaurants."

"Losing money?" Grant looked toward Susan.

"You betcha," Pete said. His laughter was hollow. "There are too many good places to eat in Denver. After I pay my suppliers and employees, I'm barely scraping by. Business is worse than it's been in years."

Since Susan was familiar with the accounts for this restaurant, she knew her father was exaggerating. He would never have to take up residence in the poorhouse, but he didn't have much liquid cash. The bulk of his wealth was tied up in investments and operations.

It hadn't occurred to her that Pete Falcone didn't have the funds to cover the ransom. If he couldn't, how in the world was she going to get her hands on that kind of money?

Chapter Seven

Defeated, Susan felt her energy desert her. She was exhausted. They'd come all this way, had stolen an airplane, and risked the weather and the darkness. All for nothing. If what her father said was true, there wasn't enough money for the ransom.

Her legs felt too weak to stand, and she sagged against the desk. If her father didn't have the funds, what could she do? Where could she go? How could she rescue Michael?

"Susan!" Carolyn's voice cracked like a whip. "You look tired, dear."

"Very tired." She nodded.

"Pull yourself together." Her mother reached out, stroked Susan's cheek and tilted her chin so that their eyes met. Carolyn's voice held steely determination as she said, "I know exactly what you need, and I'll get it for you."

What did she mean? The ransom money?

Calmly, Carolyn turned toward her husband. "Why don't you and Grant go open that bottle of wine you mentioned?"

"Susan comes, too," Pete said. "I want to toast the happy couple."

"The excitement has been too much for her," Carolyn said. "You can see that, Pete. She looks all pooped out. I'm going to take her home with me for a second. We'll be right back."

"No way, honey," Pete responded. "I want to see the both of them, holding hands and kissing like they used to. Hey, Grant, am I going to have another grandchild? Where's my little Mike, anyhow?"

"Up in the mountains with the sitter," Carolyn said. "Really, Pete. It's too late at night for Michael to be awake."

Susan eyed her mother curiously. Once Carolyn got started, she was good at lying. Quite the hidden talent. Maybe her mother should have been a lawyer. Or a politician.

Playfully, Pete tapped Grant on the shoulder. "Are we going to have another wedding? I'm not sure what to serve at a remarriage. What do you think, Grant? Twice-baked ham? Leftovers? How about refried beans?"

"If Susan consents to marry me again, the food should be honey and cream, because our love would be sweeter and smoother the second time around."

"If?" Pete questioned. He scowled at each of them in turn. "What's this 'If'? Are you two getting back together or not?"

"Of course they are," Carolyn said.

Grant echoed, "You bet. How about that wine, Pete?"

He waved to his daughter. "Come, Susan."

"No," Carolyn said. "She's staying with me."

Her father sputtered and blustered. When Pete was happy, he wanted everybody to share his joy. When he was angry, his outbursts knew no boundary. Right now, he was in between, given his celebratory mood.

Though it was unfair to let him think she and Grant were on the verge of reconciliation, Susan had to think of the greater goal. Of Michael. "Daddy, please—"

"What's the matter?" He pulled her close and kissed her cheek. "Can't I have a drink with my baby girl?"

"Stop it," Carolyn said calmly. "I need to spend time with my daughter. We have woman things to talk over."

"Yikes!" Pete raised his hands, fending off the complicated horror of "woman things." "Then go," he said. "Grant and me, we'll be okay."

The two men left the office, and Carolyn closed the door behind them. "I feel just terrible about lying to him, but I suppose it can't be helped. We need to think of Michael, don't we?"

"But why did you send Daddy away? I need to get the money from him."

Carolyn yanked off her chef's hat and unfastened her apron strings. "Open the safe and take out whatever is inside. Then we'll go to the house and get the rest. I think I have enough."

"Mama? You?"

Still, Susan couldn't quite believe her mother. Carolyn had always stood in the background, deferring to her flamboyant husband. Pete was always the unquestioned boss. At least, it had always appeared that he was in charge.

"Open the safe," Carolyn said.

Squatting down in front of the ornately decorated, old-fashioned safe, Susan twisted the knob to numerals she knew by heart. "Mama, how much is in your savings account?"

"Restaurants are a cash business, and I started saving a long time ago. For years and years I waited tables in your father's restaurants, and I had cash in tips. When you were just a baby, I turned in my dollars and pennies for my first one-hundred-dollar bill. And I added to my savings from money I saved on the household expenses."

Her mother's thriftiness was legendary in the family. But the amount of the ransom was more than pin money saved from clipping coupons and buying secondhand.

"Also," Carolyn said, "I handled the big transactions for the family. When we sold the house in the suburbs and moved to the condo, I added to my savings. And there was money from selling cars, from income-tax returns."

Those transactions might have amounted to a decent savings account. Susan began to hope. "Exactly how much money are we talking about? In your savings account?"

"Five hundred thousand, nine hundred, seventy-three dollars and eighty-seven cents. I can have the bank wire the money to you first thing in the morning."

"You have over half a million dollars in a savings account?"

"Five hundred thousand, nine hundred, seventy—"

"Why didn't you tell me before?"

"You never asked." She shrugged. "As soon as your father came in the door, I knew we couldn't reason with him. I knew what I needed to do."

In wonderment, Susan gaped, slack-jawed, at her mother, a woman who had never seemed to have any concern beyond wiping noses and bandaging scraped knees.

"Don't look so shocked," Carolyn said.

"But I've underestimated you, Mama. I'm sorry."

"Don't be." She gestured brusquely. "Hurry with the safe."

Susan opened the steel door and reached inside. "All these years, it's been you taking care of us. Tuitions for college. Down payments for cars. It was you."

"Your father and I are partners."

"But you just sat there quietly and let Dad get all the applause. Why?"

"Your father has always been adventurous with money. That's why he's a good entrepreneur. He takes risks."

"And you?"

"I keep us safe," she said. "I'm not as optimistic as your father. So, I've always saved for the rainy days."

"Thank God." Susan's heart swelled with gratitude. "Because I'm standing in a downpour, Mama."

"Then I'll be your umbrella. That's what a mother is for."

AT HALF PAST TEN, Susan and Grant returned to the airport with an old suitcase, packed with cash that her mother had taken from two restaurants and the wall safe in her home. Nearly fifty thousand dollars. And the rest would be wired to the Pinedale bank at eight o'clock the next morning. Amazing! Susan was simply amazed. Her mother's self-sufficiency revealed a side to the Falcone women that she'd taken for granted and never discussed: their strength.

They had to be strong. Each of them had chosen to marry a tough, rugged, intractable man.

At the Tech Center airfield, her brother had taken care of all the preflight details and refueling, so they were able to go directly to Sven Dahlberg's Cessna.

"Be careful," her brother warned. "The weather's getting bad in the mountains."

"Wind shear?" she asked.

"Wind. Snow. Ice. I'm not sure you can handle this. Let me come with you. I'll fly the plane."

The stolen plane? It was far better not to involve her brother. "I can do it."

"You've never flown in these conditions. Promise me that if the blizzard hits, you'll come back to Denver."

Returning wasn't an option. She and Grant needed to be back in Rampart to deal with the kidnappers. But she couldn't explain that to her brother. Instead, she nodded assurance and gave him a hug. "We'll be fine."

She stepped back to watch as he and Grant exchanged a manly embrace. They didn't say anything about having missed each other. Men didn't seem to need verbal expression of their emotions. Apparently, it was enough for them to know that they shared a history. Leave the keeping of the memories to Susan, whose heart stung with nostalgia. She remembered seeing these two men together at her wedding when her brother had been a skinny nineteen-year-old, looking awkward in his usher's tuxedo. Since that time, he'd already been through his own marriage and divorce.

The takeoff from Denver was simple, and the Cessna soared to a high altitude, above the clouds, close to the moon and stars.

"I've always liked the Falcones," Grant said. "They remind me of what a real family should be."

"Not like you and me," she said.

He ignored her dig. "I can't believe your mother had all that money socked away. On the other hand, it makes perfect sense."

"How?"

"Think about it, Susan. Your father and mother are a lot like we used to be."

"A totally, one-hundred-percent traditional marriage?" She frowned. "I don't see it."

"When we started work on Pinedale, you were the conservative one. Remember when I wanted to put a twelve-tiered waterfall in the lobby?"

"I remember."

"You didn't tell me I was an idiot."

"That's what I was thinking," she said.

"But you didn't say it."

In the small cockpit, he gestured emphatically, and she wondered how much wine Grant and her father had shared.

"You let me have my dreams," Grant continued. "Then you showed me how we could get the fountain effect without the water. You're a lot like your mother. Wise and strong."

"Me?"

That wasn't the way she remembered things. Susan had always been the queen of compromise. It had been easy to rely on Grant, and she'd allowed the big problems to rest upon his shoulders—along with the smaller problems. In the shelter of his protection, she'd avoided conflict and opted for security.

"I was always content to be the woman behind the man."

"Were you?"

He touched her arm, and she felt his warmth penetrate through the layers of her parka, sweater and turtleneck. He seemed to glow, to radiate life-giving heat. "I counted on you for everything, Grant. You were my rock, my strength, my heart. I gave everything to you."

"I never asked—"

"You didn't need to. I wanted it that way. I wanted you to be the hero and I would be a pretty princess." In this age of assertiveness and equality, it was pathetic to realize how thoroughly she'd depended upon him. After the fire, when he'd withdrawn his constant attention, she'd crumbled. "Being a princess is boring."

"You're not boring now," he said. "You can fly an airplane, put your hands on hundreds of thousands of dollars, and run a restaurant. You're doing well."

"Thank you," she said.

"Are you happy?"

His words echoed inside her like a condemnation. Could she ever be completely happy without Grant? Was there any point to her achievements and accomplishments when he wasn't there to share those moments?

She didn't want to answer those questions. Not now. Not until she held Michael safe in her arms, and her world had returned to its normal rotation.

The tiny Cessna sped through the night, propelling them toward an uncertain future. Over the mountains, the plane dipped in dancing winds that swooped and swirled. Below them, the snow-covered landscape was all but invisible through the clouds.

"We're getting there," he said. Peering down through the window, through a break in the clouds, he saw familiar landmarks. "There's Rabbit Ears Pass."

"How can you tell?"

"I know this land. We're going to make it."

Grant alternated between watching the dials on the console and the exhaustion that had begun to show on Susan's face as she navigated by instrument, following the flight maps Sven had used for this route. Her eyelids seemed heavy, and she squinted. Fiercely, her fingers gripped the yoke, holding a steady course. It looked to him like she was at the ragged end of her stamina.

When he touched her arm, she reacted, startled. "What is it, Grant?"

"Let me take over."

"I can do it," she insisted.

"You don't have to prove anything to me. It's almost midnight, and you can barely keep your eyes open."

"If I thought I could sleep, I would." Through the microphone in the headset, her voice sounded distant. "I can't sleep until this is over. I'm afraid of my dreams."

"Just relax for a minute," he said. "You'll need to be alert for the landing."

"Okay." She lifted her hands from the yoke. "Be my guest. No heroics, Grant. Try not to run into a mountain."

The plane jolted slightly as he took over the controls and rudder pedals. "How much longer?"

"You sound like Michael." She leaned back in the seat and allowed her eyelids to drop closed. "Are we there yet? He always says that on car trips. 'Are we there? How many more minutes?'"

"He likes to keep track," Grant said. "Does he still have his Saturn Patrol wristwatch?"

"It's not broken yet."

The Saturn Patrol had been Michael's favorite crew of superheroes for the past six months, and Grant would be glad when this phase was over. The mighty patrol didn't rank high in popularity, and it was near impossible to find action figures and videos. "Where did you locate the watch?"

"At an after-Christmas sale in a heap of reduced toys. I grabbed it, bought it, and Michael loves the thing. Most of the expensive toys he got for Christmas are already ruined or stashed away in his toy box. But that five-dollar wristwatch is still ticking."

"Tomorrow," Grant said firmly, "he can show me the watch. He'll be back with us."

A ribbon of silence furled between them. Uppermost in both of their minds was Michael. Was he all right? Would he be safe?

A heavy sigh puffed through her full lips. Her complexion had faded to a pale monochrome outlined by her raven black hair. Her thick eyelashes formed delicate crescents on her cheeks. So lovely. She was a princess—a beautiful, strong princess.

Over the headset, he heard a burst of static and a ground warning about bad weather. Not that Grant needed the National Weather Service to tell him about the impending snowfall.

The clouds churned and roiled below them, as threatening as an ocean undertow. Tailwinds that had aided their trip to Denver blew against them now, and it was slow going as the propellers struggled against fierce gusts.

Usually, in the midst of a rescue, he could sense the outcome, the success or failure of a mission. A surge of adrenaline would push him farther and faster, racing toward the victims who had a chance of being saved. He almost always knew if the victim would be dead or alive.

Now, he had no clue. Desperately he wanted to believe that Michael would survive. But he had no reassurance, no feeling of certainty.

Beside him, in the pilot's chair, Susan roused. She checked the instruments. "It's time to take her down."

"Can you do it?"

"I don't have a choice."

With Susan back at the controls, the Cessna plunged into the thick cloud-cover. They were flying blind. If she went too low, they would crash into the forests surrounding Rampart. If she was too high, landing would be impossible. Utterly surrounded by gray fog, buffeted by unpredictable air currents, they descended.

"Turn on the runway lights, Grant. I need something to aim for."

He dialed the radio frequencies the way Jack Slade had taught him. "The lights are on."

"I can't see," Susan whispered. "I've never done this before."

"You'll make it."

"We're too low. I should take her up again."

But she kept going down, down through heavy moisture that coated the windows and laid ice upon the wings. If the plane crashed, it meant certain death for them. And for Michael? What would happen to their son? "Keep going, Susan."

When they passed through the clouds, the weather cleared to a thin haze. The snow was not yet falling. They were skimming the treetops.

"Look!" Grant pointed. He could see the faraway glow from street lamps and porch lights in Rampart. And the runway. Grant sighted the parallel strips of faint lights. "We're almost there."

But she was coming in too fast. Susan cut her speed. The altimeter sank precipitously on this short approach. The descent seemed like a dive as the runway rose up to meet them. And Grant held his breath, poised between sky and earth, between safety and disaster, life and death.

The Cessna's wheels touched down in a rough, heavy landing. They jolted in their seats, but Susan held on.

He exhaled with a triumphant shout. "You did it!"

She taxied to a stop, only skidding for a few yards. She peeled her hands from the yoke, tore off her headset and turned to him with a radiant smile.

"You're one hell of a pilot, Susan Richardson."

"Damn right."

There had been a time when he would have taken her into his arms and expressed his joy and gratitude with a kiss. Now, he had to be satisfied with words. "I'm proud of you."

"Two years ago, I would have given my left arm to hear you say those words." She laughed, and the sound was tinged with brittleness. "Maybe my right arm."

"I was always proud."

"Sure. Whatever." She sighed and stared through the windshield. "Why don't you drive this plane into the hangar?"

He took over the controls. "Two years ago...was I really that cold?"

"A world-class workaholic. You made Donald Trump look like a sensitive guy."

He knew her complaints. He'd heard them so many times. Insensitive. Distant. Uncaring. Obsessed with his work. His counselors had repeated the labels for him. "Emotionally unavailable," he said.

"Emotionally and physically. We only made love four times in that year after the fire."

"Are you sure?" He couldn't believe that he'd lain beside this beautiful, desirable woman every night and hadn't touched her.

"I'm positively certain," she said. "I marked each occasion in my desk calendar with a big red heart."

The thought of her marking her calendar touched him. At the same time, he was appalled by his own lack of awareness. He'd truly had no idea how much he'd hurt her. Talk about a selfish bastard. "I told you, didn't I? I'm sorry."

"Yes," she said.

"When, Susan? When are you going to forgive me?"

"I don't know." She blinked and looked away from him. "I don't know if I can forgive."

He would teach her how. Tonight, he would show her that he could be the man she once had loved.

When Michael was back with them again, they would be a family.

Working quickly, they returned Sven Dahlberg's plane to the hangar, only slightly worse for wear. Grant led the way to Slade's Adventures and slipped the extra key back into the desk drawer.

So far, so good. They had the ransom money. They were safe. For the first time since he'd seen Susan skiing alone toward Slade's Adventures, he felt confident. Everything was going to be all right.

He slung his backpack over his shoulder. "Let's go."

The overhead light in the office flicked on, momentarily blinding them. Sven Dahlberg stood beside the door with his hand on the switch. "Not so fast, Grant."

"What are you doing here?"

"What the hell were you doing with my plane? I'm going to have you arrested. Both of you."

But Grant didn't see the sheriff. If Sven had intended to put them in jail, he would have brought Walt Perkins with him. "What do you want, Sven?"

"You know what I'm after."

"Pinedale," Grant said. He wasn't in the mood for threats. Sven had better watch out.

"After this little incident, you're screwed. You might as well go along with me, save yourself the embarrassment of jail time."

"I can explain," Grant said. He placed his backpack on Jack Slade's desk and flipped it open. "I have something in here that should make everything crystal clear."

"No excuses. Give me what I want. Or else."

Grant raised his handgun to Sven's eye level. "Or else what?"

Susan stepped in front of him. "Grant, no! Don't kill him."

The thought hadn't occurred to Grant. Kill him? He didn't want to kill Sven or anyone else. He wasn't a murderer.

It was Sven who said, "He won't shoot me. Grant's the big rescue man. He saves people."

"Not this time," Susan said darkly.

She knew Grant would never pull the trigger. But if Sven didn't believe he was in danger, he could cause a lot of trouble. She wouldn't let that happen. Her mother wasn't the only one who could pull off a deception.

Infusing her voice with emotion wasn't difficult. She was already near the breaking point—so near that the tremble in her throat was real. "You've got to believe me. Something terrible has happened, and Grant isn't himself. He scares me. And he should scare you, too."

Sven's blond eyebrows lowered in a disbelieving scowl. He was a tall man with an air of self-importance. His lip curled with disdain as he asked, "What happened?"

"You tell me," she said. "About Michael."

"Who?" His confusion appeared to be real. "Who the hell is Michael?"

"Our son," she said.

"What about him? I know Grant has a kid, but what's the big deal?"

"He's been kidnapped," she said. "Grant thought you might know something about it."

"Me?" His voice was a high-pitched squeak. A

shimmer of fear dawned in his cold blue eyes. "You think I kidnapped your son?"

"Don't lie to us. I warn you, Sven, my ex-husband is insane with grief. If you don't tell us what we need to know, he will kill you."

"I don't know anything." He waved his hands in front of his face. "Kidnapping is a federal offense. I wouldn't get mixed up in anything like that."

Grant chimed in. His voice was harsh. "What about the money? The ransom. What do you know about that?"

"Nothing. I swear."

With the gun held out straight in front of him, Grant came around the desk. "Tell me. Or you die slow."

Sven shook his head. No words came from his mouth.

"Tell me about Bart O'Dell."

"O'Dell? He's done some work for me." He licked his lips. "You wouldn't really hurt me."

"Don't try me, Sven."

Again, Susan stepped in. "I think he's telling the truth."

"I don't trust him," Grant said. "There's cord in my backpack. Tie his hands behind his back."

"You don't have to do that," Sven pleaded. "Look, I'll forget about the plane. No harm done. Just let me go."

"Shut up!" Grant roared. "I don't want to hear your voice. Either you be quiet and cooperate, or I'll hurt you. Real bad."

He was so forceful that Susan almost believed him. But she knew Grant's attitude wasn't all playacting. He must truly despise this man who had caused so much trouble for him, fanning the flames of past hatreds.

She tied Sven's trembling hands behind his back, using climber's knots that Grant had taught her.

"How did you know about the plane?" Grant demanded.

"I got a call. Anonymous. It was a man. He said there was something going on at Slade's Adventures, and I might want to check on my Cessna."

"Must have been the kidnapper," Susan said.

That meant they were still in the area, watching and waiting. But why would they contact Sven? The kidnapper must have understood that they were taking the plane so they could get the ransom money.

She stepped away from Sven. "He's done."

"Pat him down. See if he has a weapon."

She did so and found nothing. "Grant, why would the kidnappers cause this kind of problem for us? They must have known that we were going after the ransom."

"Maybe the money isn't all that important," he said.

"They didn't ask for anything else. What are they after?"

"Revenge." He turned to Sven and said, "I want you to give Melanie a call so she won't worry about you."

"What am I going to tell her?"

"The truth." Grant didn't relax his grip on the gun. "Tell her that you're to have the honor of being my first guest at Pinedale."

THEY'D GOTTEN SVEN locked into one of the first-floor rooms, and Grant didn't feel the least bit guilty about leaving him there on the bed with his hands and feet securely tied to the bedposts.

He came back into the lobby where Susan had collapsed on a chair. The suitcase full of money rested between her feet.

"Sven's not going anywhere," he stated bluntly.

"I'm sorry we had to take him. But there was no way we could turn him loose."

"No way at all." He sat beside her. "What now, Susan? Do you want to rest?"

"I'm going to try. And you?"

"Same."

There was only one telephone call on the message machine. Grant played it back so they both could listen.

"Susan?" It was her mother's voice. "Call me at home when you get in. No matter how late. I'm worried."

In the brief pause that followed, Grant heard a soft sighing. He deeply regretted any pain he might have caused Carolyn Falcone.

She continued, "Susan, do you think the kidnapping had anything to do with your father? I hate to think so, but the Falcones have many enemies. Please call."

"What do you think?" Susan asked. "Were the kidnappers trying to extort the ransom from my father?"

"If this were a professional job, I'd say your father was the likely target. But these guys aren't pros. They've made too many stupid mistakes. Like calling Sven. And when they pushed the Jeep off the road, they didn't hide it. Professional criminals wouldn't do anything as stupid as stealing O'Dell's truck for their getaway. And, of course, there's the money.''

''What about the money?''

''It's a weird amount. The same amount as the insurance payoff. And it's not enough.''

''Four hundred and fifty thousand seems like plenty to me.''

''Think about it, Susan. Kidnapping is a federal crime. As soon as we get Michael back, we'll call in the FBI and anybody else who can catch these kidnappers. Anybody who takes that kind of risk is going to ask for a million. Besides, if they were after your father, they wouldn't have advised you to wait here at Pinedale with me. I think they would have struck in Denver, where your father could easily lay hands on the cash.''

''Then why? Revenge?''

''I hate to think about it.''

''Me, too.''

Grant was sure that Susan's father wasn't the focus of the crime. ''Give your mother a call and try to put her mind at rest. Even if she's right and the kidnappers are trying to extort money from your father, it's not Pete's fault. Nor is it your fault or mine. The kidnappers are the criminals. Not us. We can't start blaming each other.''

''You're right, Grant.'' She headed toward the phones to call her mother. ''And, by the way, that's a very sensitive perception.''

''I have my moments,'' he said.

But not too many of them. Sensitivity wasn't his strongest trait. He was better at handling an overt crisis, like an avalanche. And he'd always been that way. Even when he was a full-time lawyer, he preferred the cut-and-dried factual evidence of a case. Only occasionally did he manage to guess at motivation, and he never trusted the testimony of expert witnesses in the so-called psychological sciences.

Susan was yawning when she got off the telephone. "I think Mama's okay. As good as can be expected."

"I'm sorry we had to put her through this."

"It's awful for her. Mama has endured so much pain and frustration from me. All my mistakes. All the times I've botched up my life."

"What about your successes?"

"There haven't been many," she said.

"Do I hear the rumblings of low self-esteem?"

She eyed him curiously. "This newfound sensitivity of yours, I like it."

"Thanks."

She yawned again. "Where should I sleep?"

He saw a question in her eyes, and he tried to read what she was really thinking. Was she asking if she should sleep in his bed? He dared not imagine the sweetness of that possibility. He'd already made his uneasy truce with the fact that she would never sleep with him again. Never again would he see her silken black hair spread across a white pillowcase. Never again would he reach over and touch her supple flesh. Nor inhale the warm fragrance of her body.

And yet, he whispered, "Sleep beside me, Susan. My bed will always be yours."

Her gentle hazel eyes, more gray than green, regarded him with an odd intensity, as if she were actually considering his proposal. For an instant, his spirits took flight. She might relent, might loosen her grip on the overwhelming resentment that had destroyed their love.

"Please," he urged. Sensitivity or humility? He was begging, willing to sacrifice every shred of his pride for reconciliation. "If you don't want me to touch you, I won't. Please, Susan, lie beside me."

Chapter Eight

Grant waited for her answer. He'd taken a chance. He'd spoken. Now the reply was up to her.

She sighed. "I can't go to bed with you, Grant."

His hopes exploded, blown away by the gentle whisper of her voice. "Of course not," he said. "What the hell was I thinking?"

The tension he felt in his gut needed no translation by a counselor. He wanted her with his whole heart and soul. But he could never have her.

"The ransom money." She pointed toward it. "Where should we put it?"

"I have a safe in the office," he said.

"Is it big enough for this satchel?"

"It's the size of a small walk-in closet. This is a hotel, you know."

He picked up the bag, went into the office and closed the door. Glad to be away from her, still angered by her latest rejection, he took care of the money and sank down in the chair behind his desk. Damn, he was a fool. When was he going to accept the fact that she was never going to forgive him?

He heard a tap on the door. "What?"

She poked her head in the door. "Where should I sleep, Grant?"

"There are over a hundred beds at Pinedale. Take your pick."

"Well, I'm sure you don't have sheets on all the beds, and I don't know—"

"I'll tell you what, Susan, I'll give you some blankets and you can hole up in the far-north wing, second floor, at the very end. That's a long way from here. You could sing to yourself and turn up the television full blast. I'd never even know you were there."

"I want to be closer to the telephone." Her tone was clipped, terse, snappish. "Obviously."

He responded in kind. "Obviously."

The chill factor froze the atmosphere between them. Her fine features were now sculpted in ice. Their brief flicker of affection had died a cold, hypothermic death.

He led her to the concierge's room nearest the front desk. Once he got Pinedale rolling, he would have a full-time employee who lived on the premises and took care of details. Right now, he couldn't afford a concierge. He pushed open the door. "You can stay here. This bed is all made up."

"And where will you be?"

"Don't worry. I won't attack you," he said coolly. "Sven is the only other guest in the hotel and, pardon the pun, he's all tied up."

Fleeing from potential argument, he crossed the lobby and stood beside an unmarked, closed door. "If you need anything, my apartment is over here. It's just the way we designed it in the blueprints. Not that I expect you to remember."

"Of course I remember. We wanted to be sure we could live at the hotel and still have our privacy."

He pushed open the door. "I don't suppose you want to have a look around."

"Wrong," she said. Briskly, she walked past him. "I spent a lot of time poring over those plans. I have a right to see how it all turned out."

"Afraid I made a mess of it?"

"I'm just curious."

Grant was proud of the way their plans had turned out. His private apartment was among the last of the renovations, but he hadn't stinted. Nor had he made any modifications to the blueprints Susan had approved two years ago.

He followed her into the small entryway, which formed a buffer against the lobby noise. There was a living-room and dining-room combination with a fireplace. Down a hallway was a master bedroom, Michael's room and another small bedroom. The galley-style kitchen was furnished with top-of-the-line appliances that he didn't really appreciate. Susan had always done the cooking, and he'd never developed the knack.

As she moved silently through the apartment they should have shared, he waited for her opinion. There was no way she couldn't like the place. But would she give him the satisfaction of admitting that she was impressed?

In the kitchen, she ran her fingertips over the gleaming, almond-colored stovetop. The sound she made in the back of her throat was almost a purr. Or maybe a growl? He didn't know what she was thinking or imagining anymore.

She returned to the front room and arranged herself on the sofa in front of the hearth. "Gas fireplace?"

"Yes."

"This is beautiful, Grant. May I ask who selected the furnishings?"

"You did."

"Me?"

"Don't you remember? You made a scrapbook of colors, styles and designs. I liked the way it looked."

Curiously, she stared up at him. "I didn't think you even noticed my scrapbook."

"I noticed everything you did. Every gesture. Every suggestion. Especially in the kitchen."

"Because I'm a master chef?" She repeated their old joke.

"And a damn good cook."

Two round spots of color appeared on her cheeks. She seemed softer, more contented.

"If it's not too much trouble," she said, "I'd like to see the kitchen for the coffee shop and restaurant."

"Follow me."

Toward the rear of the hotel, he led the way from the lobby through beveled-glass-paned French doors to a terra-cotta-tiled hallway. To the left was a cheery-looking coffee shop with booths, round maple tables and blue gingham curtains. Grant went through to the kitchen where he turned on the overhead lights of the coffee shop. "I had to modify our plans and take out some of the windows. Not only do we lose too much heat, but the only view from this side is the dog enclosure and a road leading around to the kitchen for deliveries. Building on the edge of a riverbank required some adaptations."

"I love it, Grant. It's charming."

"Back here is the kitchen."

This was where the fire had been. After he had the insurance money in hand, Grant had given up on saving any portion of the original structure, except the basement and wine cellar. The kitchen was all modern, all new. And Susan seemed delighted with the arrangements.

Her hostility evaporated as she buzzed around the kitchen, commenting on how well the various suggestions she'd made so long ago had worked. Without thinking, she picked up a sponge from one of the sinks and began wiping crumbs from a stainless-steel countertop.

"I wish my father could see this," she said. "He's always telling me that my ideas are too expensive. Were they?"

"I'm broke," he said. "But it's worth every penny."

If for no other reason than to see the light of approval on her lovely face, he was glad that he'd put in the extra effort. "Sometimes being a perfectionist pays off."

"I never said that it didn't." Her smile was teasing. "But it's still an annoying trait."

"Does that make me a creep? Or a hero?"

"A heroic creep." At the end of the stainless-steel countertops and work area, she nodded toward a closed door near the rear exit. "Does this lead to the wine cellar?"

"It does, but we don't need to bother going down there. I don't have much in the way of stock."

"I know just the person to help you with selection and pricing. She's absolutely brilliant at finding unusual domestic wines." She touched a cabinet-size, stainless-steel sliding door that was flush with the wall. "And this is the dumbwaiter to the wine cellar. You even incorporated that idea."

Actually, that had been one of her better inspirations. "I needed it to move wine and champagne by the crate. The dumbwaiter is bigger than we'd originally planned. A mini-elevator, really, large enough to use for sending trays of food upstairs to the ballroom."

Her eyes flashed wide. "Oh, Grant! You re-created the ballroom?"

The fire had destroyed the original, ornately decorated ballroom. When they first began planning the reconstruction after the fire, the ballroom had seemed to be an unnecessary expense.

"It wasn't as costly as I'd thought," Grant said. "And it's a great space for wedding receptions and banquets. I even added a couple of meeting rooms along one side."

"I have to see this."

Without needing to be told the way, Susan charged up a back stairway that led from the kitchen to the ballroom on the second floor.

Her enthusiasm pleased him. Was he crazy? Why couldn't he just hate her and forget? Every chance she got, Susan flayed his pride, taking him for a ride on an emotional roller coaster. If he let her call every shot, he was no kind of man at all.

Yet, in her presence, he felt one-hundred-percent virile. She was his mate. Whether he liked it or not, this was their home. Pinedale had meant a lot to them. The hotel had been the center of their lives, and the fire had been their undoing.

He followed her up the stairway. "Wait a minute."

She paused outside the door, lit by the red glow of an exit sign. So excited that she fidgeted, she was unbelievably cute. There was bright excitement in her eyes, a Christmas-morning sense of anticipation.

Playing with a set of wall switches, he adjusted the lighting and held open the doors for her. Beneath chandeliers and matching wall sconces, the parquet floor glistened. The color scheme was a mellow gold with burgundy trim that matched the curtains. Grant had tried to recapture the rococo style of the original. It was a huge space with a player piano, given to them by Grant's mother, a music teacher, as a wedding present.

While Susan explored the room, commenting with sheer delight on the details he'd managed to copy, he went to the player piano, made a selection and turned it on. The music was "A Summer Place." Once, it had been their song.

He came to her. "One dance. For old times' sake."

"I'd like that."

Her hand felt warm and soft in his. Lightly he grasped her waist, keeping a proper distance between them. So many nights, he'd dreamed of this moment. As they moved together to the music, their bodies naturally came closer and closer, until they were almost touching.

"The first time we danced to this song," she remembered, "it was playing on a jukebox in a little neighborhood bar in Denver."

"I was still a lawyer back then," he said.

"And I wasn't impressed by your profession."

"You called me a barracuda."

"Only after I told you I worked at a restaurant as

a chef, and you stupidly informed me that the greatest chefs were men.''

''Some sensitivity, huh?''

When she laughed, the lovely noise pealed like distant chimes across a green and sunlit meadow. As he embraced her, they generated enough heat to melt the January blizzard. The cruel night softened into a seductive pastel haze.

''I always wondered, after that lousy first impression, why did you agree to go out with me?'' he asked.

''You were genuine, and I was sick of men who pretended to be understanding but really weren't.'' Her eyes sparkled. ''And why did you ask for a date?''

''Because you were the most beautiful woman I'd ever seen.''

Still beautiful, but so much more. She was the only woman for him. The mother of his son. His wife. Susan was intelligent and brave. Perhaps he had counted too much on her strength, believing she would endure his insensitivity.

The song was coming to an end. He pulled her a bit closer, and she winced. ''Are you all right?''

''It's nothing. I was injured a little bit. By the kidnappers.''

''You never told me.''

''I've had a few other things on my mind.''

Instantly concerned, he stepped away from her. ''Pull up your turtleneck so I can take a look.''

''That's not necessary, Grant.''

''I have my first-aid kit downstairs, and you know I'm an expert at patching people up.''

''No,'' she said firmly.

The music died.

"Tell me what happened. How were you hurt?"

She turned her back. Through the fabric of her turtleneck, he saw the outline of her graceful spine. "It's nothing serious. One of the men kicked me in the ribs."

White-hot anger exploded inside Grant. It hadn't occurred to him that she might be physically hurt. Tersely he said, "Show me."

"I'd rather not."

"Come on, Susan. You've been injured, and I can make you more comfortable."

Carefully she untucked her turtleneck from the waistband of her jeans and lifted up the soft cotton fabric to the lower edge of her bra. Her pale torso gleamed in the soft ballroom light. Like an obscene tattoo, a purple-and-yellow bruise discolored the left side of her rib cage.

When he touched the darkened area, she sucked in her breath, holding back her complaint.

"Bastards," he muttered.

"It's not that bad," she said. "I hardly notice it. No big deal. It happened when I fought back. The shorter man shoved me to the ground. He tried to strangle me, and he kicked me while I was down."

If Grant ever found these guys, he would kill them. Holding himself in tight control, he said, "We'll get you some aspirin. You should soak in a hot tub. I have a cold pack and a heating pad. We'll alternate the two. As soon as possible, we'll get that bruise X-rayed to see if the ribs are cracked."

"It's not necessary," she said.

"Let me take care of you, Susan."

"I'll be fine."

He ignored her protests. "Where else were you injured? Is there anyplace else you feel pain?"

"Here." She clutched her hands at her breast. "In my heart."

He met her gaze, knowing exactly what she was thinking.

"Damn it, Grant. If they did this to me, what could they be doing to Michael? He's only a little boy. What if he tries to get away and they—"

"Hush." He pulled her close against him, not wanting to face the horrifying possibility that the kidnappers might abuse his son. If those bastards had harmed one hair on Michael's head, Grant vowed he would track them to the ends of the earth and make them pay a hundredfold for his son's pain.

She trembled against him, quaking like the last golden aspen leaves before the winter storms. "I can't stand not knowing, Grant. I feel so helpless."

"I know." He stroked her back, trying to soothe her and knowing that the terror went beyond comforting. "Damn it, I know."

He could feel her tension, the unbearable fear of a mother who could not protect her child.

For several minutes, they stood together, sharing a dark and horrible tension. All night, he'd been hoping to touch her, to feel her body against his. Now, while he held her, making love was the furthest thing from his mind.

He was caught in the tight grip of impotent terror. Someone had taken his son. Michael might be suffering, and there wasn't a damn thing Grant could do to help him. This had to be the worst pain anyone could inflict upon a father.

TOMORROW, HIS REVENGE would be complete.

Though the kid was still asleep, he changed the videotape in the VCR. Saturn Patrol? What a load of crap! Only a kid could believe in magical superheroes with Saturn rings around their heads. Real soon, little Mikey would find out that nobody could save the world—especially not his daddy.

Tomorrow, this would be over. Maybe then, he could sleep peacefully and wake up refreshed.

Maybe then, all the color would come back into his world.

Carefully, he unwrapped the small bouquet he'd carried with him. Rachel had loved flowers, and he knew she would have enjoyed these blossoms he'd fashioned from paper. Red and yellow roses, of course. The symbolism was obvious. Mingled among them was a white spray of forget-me-nots. Another symbol.

Grant would never forget, never.

Though his carefully laid plans hadn't gone exactly as intended, the end result would be the same.

Grant's life would be destroyed.

And Susan—sweet, pretty Susan—would die. A single red rose would mark her grave. Forget-me-not.

BY THE TIME GRANT had showered and gotten into bed, it was after two o'clock in the morning—eight hours until the time when the kidnappers had said they would call.

"Exhausted" was a mild description of how he felt. Though he'd often had more physically rigorous days, he couldn't recall any time in his life when he'd suffered such prolonged, severe stress. His muscles ached from being held taut. His brain hurt from asking questions for which there might be no answers.

He lay back on the pillows and tried to relax. His pulse pounded heavily, and with each beat, he longed for his son. The pressure of Michael's absence was more agonizing than ever before.

And then, there was Susan.

Occasionally, during this miserable day, their usual barrage of hostilities and barbs had ceased. He'd seen her as she once had been: trusting, loving and loyal. The vision of their distant past tormented him, mocking him with false hope for a future together.

When he closed his eyes, he saw her lovely face. His fingers itched to touch her silky hair. His body shuddered with need for her.

What the hell was wrong with him? They were divorced. Each time he'd held out his hand toward her, she'd rebuffed him. She'd made it clear that she wanted nothing to do with him. Not now. Not ever.

His marriage was gone. And his son...

Though Grant wouldn't have thought it possible, he must have slept in dreamless slumber, because when he looked again at the bedside clock, it was 6:00 a.m. Four hours until the kidnappers' call.

For about twelve seconds, he considered trying to return to sleep. But he was wide-awake, itching for this to be over. Grant bolted from the bed. The need for action burned within him.

After he dressed, he left his private apartment and entered the lobby. As always, he silently greeted the portrait of Susan that hung there. The frame was slightly askew, as if her presence had dislodged his memories. He straightened the picture and headed toward the first-floor room where he'd left Sven.

As soon as Grant pushed open the door, he heard loud snoring. Being tied to the bed with long ropes hadn't hampered Sven's ability to snooze, and the fact that he was able to sleep disproved the adage, No rest for the wicked.

Though Grant was sure that Sven had nothing to do with Michael's kidnapping, he still didn't like or trust the developer. Raping the environment for his condo building was bad enough, but Sven had also put a couple of ranchers out of business, buying up their land.

Change was good. It meant progress. But the citizens of Rampart needed to be cautious instead of greedy, or else their community would turn into a blight of ugly convenience stores and supermarkets. The charm would be gone.

Wistfully, Grant wondered if he might be smart to sell Pinedale to Dahlberg Enterprises and move on. He wasn't really an innkeeper. With Susan and Michael gone, the running of the hotel wouldn't be much fun.

He closed the door to Sven's room and went toward the kitchen. He might attempt to cook a full breakfast. At least, it would use up some time.

In the Pinedale coffee shop, he saw light coming from the kitchen. The redolent aroma of brewed coffee wafted in the air. Perfect coffee. Nobody made coffee the way Susan did.

She was busy in the kitchen, humming tunelessly. On the stainless-steel counter were a dozen fresh baked cinnamon rolls and a braided strudel.

So many times he'd imagined those fragrances, that warmth, and the fond satisfaction of watching her skillful fingers working in dough. "Susan?"

Sheepishly, she glanced at him. "I couldn't sleep."

He gestured at the baked goods. "I can tell. Baking always made you feel better."

"It's productive. When I'm baking, I feel like I'm doing something."

Under a white bib apron, she wore her jeans and one of his turtlenecks. It was a bright red that enhanced the flush in her cheeks. His shirt was, of course, too big, and she bunched the sleeves up past her elbows.

He remembered last night and the harsh bruises she'd not seen fit to mention. "How are you feeling?"

"How do you think?" she asked sarcastically. "I'm nervous, scared, panicked. Maybe a little hysterical—"

"Your ribs," he interrupted. Grant didn't need a rundown of her psychological ills, which had to be similar to his own. "How are your injuries?"

She touched her ribs, leaving a handprint of white flour on the red turtleneck. "It's just a bruise. If they were cracked, I'd have a lot more discomfort."

"Let me make breakfast," he offered. "You can relax."

"You? Cooking? No, thanks." Like the unquestioned queen of the kitchen, she brandished a wooden spoon like a scepter. "Would you like an omelet? Crepes? Sausage?"

Grant was glad to relent. "Whatever you feel like making."

After her whirlwind of culinary efficiency, they sat at a table in the coffee shop, forcing themselves to take one delicious bite after another. It was a shame to let her cooking go to waste, but neither of them felt like eating. They didn't speak of Michael or the kidnappers, but their awareness was heavy and certain.

"I was thinking," Susan said as she pushed a piece of omelet around on her plate. "Why did the kidnappers contact Sven and tell him about the plane?"

"Maybe they weren't the ones who telephoned him."

"Nobody else would make an anonymous call. Why, Grant? Why would the kidnappers get in our way while we were trying to gather the ransom?"

"It doesn't make a lot of sense." But neither did the kidnapping. It was a dangerous, vicious crime, fraught with severe consequences.

"Last night, you suggested that the money wasn't all that important, that the kidnappers were looking for revenge."

"That points to Donny and Doc Evanston." She dropped her fork on the plate. "You might have been on the right track when we went there yesterday."

"I've worked with Doc on a number of rescues," he said. "After Rachel's death, we couldn't be friends. But I respect the man, and he doesn't seem crazy enough to do something like this."

"What about Donny?"

"I barely know him."

Another thought had been playing in the back of Grant's mind. The most obvious person to want revenge would be Charley Beacham, Rachel's husband. Charley had been one of Grant's best friends in law school, and he was the one who had brought them to Rampart in the first place. He'd left after Rachel's funeral, a grieving man, and Grant hadn't heard from him since.

"Oh, well," Susan said. "I guess there's nothing we can do right now. But after we have Michael back, we're going to have to direct the police investigation toward Rachel's family."

Though they took their time cleaning in the kitchen, it was only eight o'clock when they were done.

Outside, snow had begun to fall.

In the front lobby, Grant stood at a window, looking out. The sputtering little storm wasn't the blizzard that the weathermen had predicted, but it might be the prelude. Where was Michael being kept? How far away?

He glanced over his shoulder at Susan, who stood behind the front desk, her gaze riveted to the telephone switchboard.

"I'm sure he's all right," Grant said. "Randy told me he was only sleepy and was watching Saturn Patrol videos."

She nodded.

"Would you like a tour of Pinedale?" he offered. Hiking around the hotel would help pass the time. "Or you could have a workout. I put in an exercise room and sauna."

"I need to be here," she said. "By the phone."

He checked his wristwatch. Seventeen minutes after eight o'clock. "In a couple of minutes, I can leave for the bank. To pick up the cash your mother was going to wire."

"What are you going to tell them about the money?"

"I'll say it's for the hotel. For the grand opening."

"Sounds good to me," she said. "We're getting adept at lying."

Lies. Revenge. And tension. Grant couldn't stand the impotence of waiting, helpless. He had to do something. "I think I'll check in with the postmistress and see if I can get her to tell me who else lives on the road near Elephant Rock and O'Dell's cabin."

"Might as well."

He punched in the number for the Rampart Post Office. After discussing the weather with Postmistress Addie Henry, Grant said, "I have a favor to ask. Yesterday, I was up at the Old Grange Road and talked to Adrian Walker."

"Sweet woman," Addie said.

"Yes, she is. And she asked if I'd mind dropping off a coffee cake to one of her neighbors. Other things got in the way, and now I've forgotten the name. Could you tell me who else lives up there?"

"Let me see. There's the Baers and the Foxes, but their cabins are empty. A lot of empty cabins up there. Mostly the people on Old Grange are summer residents."

An empty cabin might be exactly what Grant was seeking. "Have you got a list?"

"I can do this in my head." She ran through four or five names. "Way up top in the canyon, where the light is good, there's that woman who makes quilts and that artist fellow, Rosewood. Nearer to Adrian, there's a couple of rentals. A Johnson. A MacIntire."

"Who owns the rentals?"

"People in town. Since Sven Dahlberg isn't buying up there, they can't get rid of the cabins."

Grant made a calculated guess. "Doesn't Doc Evanston own some of those rental properties?"

"Two of them. Real cute little cabins with red trim.

They only have summer water, so nobody's living there now.''

"Thanks, Addie.''

He hung up and told Susan about the conversation. This was the best lead so far. "The Evanstons have motive for revenge. And they also just happen to have vacant cabins in the area in question.''

"What should we do?''

"Go there,'' Grant said. "Find Michael and get him back.''

She considered, then shook her head. "We only have an hour and a half to wait. Let's do it their way first.''

This time, he couldn't agree. If their line of reasoning was correct, Michael wasn't being held for ransom. This was a crime of vengeance, designed to inflict the greatest hurt—an eye for an eye. The money didn't matter.

If he started right now, he could make it to the bank and Doc Evanston's cabins on Old Grange Road well before ten o'clock. His timing was perfect. The kidnappers wouldn't expect a strike before their scheduled phone call.

He went to the coatrack beside the front door, took down his parka and slipped into it.

"Grant, please.'' She'd come from behind the front desk to stand near him. "We've done everything they said. Please just pick up the money at the bank and come back here.''

Doubt peppered his mind. What if they were wrong? What if the kidnappers never intended to bring Michael back? Could Grant stop them? Should he try?

"Listen to me,'' Susan said. She placed her slender

hand on his chest, just above his heart. "Please do it my way. Don't be a hero."

The perfect oval of her face tilted up toward him. Her eyes beseeched him.

Quietly, he said, "I can't help being who I am. But I won't go to Doc Evanston's cabins unless you agree that it's the right thing."

"Thank you."

"First, I'll go to the bank and pick up the money. Then, I'll come back here. Think about what I've said. We'd still have time to get to the cabins before ten o'clock."

"I'll think about it."

When she smiled, her lips parted slightly, inviting him to taste.

Gently, he glided his arms around her and pulled her close. Her body responded to his touch.

Though Grant knew they were holding each other from mutual need, there was warmth that flowed between them. And he began to hope. There might be a spark of love, a tiny ember. If he carefully fanned the flames, the fire would grow.

He stepped back, separating himself from her. "I'll go to the bank now."

"I'll be here. Waiting."

PICKING UP four hundred thousand dollars in cash should have meant something to him, but all Grant could think of was Susan and Michael. He rushed the bank vice president through the transaction, stashing the money—all large bills—in the suitcase with the cash they'd collected last night from the restaurants.

Back in the truck, he raced to Pinedale. When he parked outside the front entry, the time was seven minutes past nine. He dashed inside and held up the suitcase so Susan could see. "It's all here."

"Thank God."

He went past her into the office, tossed the suitcase in the walk-in safe and locked it.

"Nothing," Susan said.

"Okay." He looked at his wristwatch. Twelve minutes past nine. Time was running out. "I need to take care of the dogs, then I'll be right back."

"Grant—"

"I'll want your decision then, Susan. Either we wait or we act."

He circled around behind the hotel. The skies were gunmetal gray, dotted with gently falling snow.

As he approached the chain-link enclosure, the dogs bounded up to greet him, tumbling over each other in excitement. If they sensed his portentous mood, they gave no sign. Instead, they bounced off each other as if their feet were attached to bedsprings.

Though he usually allowed them to run free in the early morning or else hitched them to the sled for exercise, today Grant didn't want to waste any time with chasing, petting or playing. He pushed inside the enclosure, wading through dogs, and went to the shed where he kept the sled and the stock of dry dog food.

Snuffy was particularly rambunctious this morning. She nudged at his leg with her nose and made urgent yips.

"I know you want to go for a run," he said. "But not today, girl."

While he prepared food and water, Snuffy stayed on his heels. A couple of times, she ran to the gate and stared out, as if she were seeing something important. Then she ran back to him. She ignored the food bowls and snapped when Pyrite tried to engage her in play. Snuffy's golden fur was trembling as she stared up at Grant, then ran again to the gate.

"Later today, we'll exercise," he promised her. "When Michael is with us."

Grant went to the gate and opened it.

Charging, Snuffy dodged around him and outside the enclosure. What was going on with her?

"Snuffy! Get back here!"

The usually obedient dog shook herself and took off at a slow lope, circling the hotel.

Grant locked the gate behind him and trailed her. The last thing he needed this morning was trouble with his animals. "Snuffy!" he shouted.

But she was gone, off on her own private quest.

At the front of the hotel, she sat poised, almost as if she were waiting for him to spot her. When she was sure that he had, she took off again.

Grant saw exactly where she was headed. Last night, she'd found something interesting near the farthest of the enclosed parking garages. No doubt Snuffy had dreamed of this hidden treasure and couldn't wait to dig it up.

And yet, as he approached, she wasn't digging in the snow. She stood at the closed garage door, staring intently. It was the position she took during their practiced avalanche rescues, when she'd found the supposed victim buried in the snow.

Apprehension raised the hairs on the nape of his neck. Yesterday, he'd given Michael's cap to Snuffy. She hadn't picked up the scent at that time. But now?

Grant joined the dog outside the closed garage door. There were no tracks in the new-fallen snow.

Was Michael inside? Had he been here all along? Last night had been frigid.

With a yank, Grant pulled up the garage door. Inside was a beat-up green Toyota truck. The vanity plates read, ODELL.

Susan Kearney 172

When Michael fell for Susan, he fell hard. Just once more, Susan smiled.

Will a year's separation and a secret threaten to keep these lovers apart? He's on tenterhooks until
he sees her again.

Chapter Nine

Susan stood behind the desk near the PBX console. Should she go to the cabins with Grant? Or should she try to stop him?

She closed her eyes, trying to visualize her son and his surroundings, but it was an image of Grant that swam before her. She heard his baritone voice saying, "Come with me."

"No." Her eyelids snapped open.

She would stay here and pay the ransom. The kidnappers would call and everything would be fine.

Through the front windows, she saw the start of the snowfall. The beginning of the blizzard?

What if Grant was right? What if Michael had been kidnapped for revenge? She couldn't imagine Doc Evanston doing such a thing. His daughter's death had caused him a great deal of pain, but he was a doctor. He'd attended at Michael's birth when her labor pains started early and they couldn't get to the hospital in time.

But what about Donny? He'd seemed hotheaded and still embittered by his sister's death.

Susan couldn't ignore the coincidences. Donny lived in Oregon, but he'd come here to Rampart.

Why? Doc Evanston owned rental cabins on the road where they knew the kidnappers had gone.

She thumbed through the slim local telephone directory and found the phone number for Doc Evanston. Before she could change her mind, she tapped out the number on the switchboard keys.

"This is Dr. Evanston."

"Hi, Doc. It's me. Susan Richardson."

"Hello, Susan. How nice to hear your voice again. My son mentioned that you and Grant dropped by yesterday."

"I'm sorry if we bothered him," she said. Was Donny there? Or was he at the rental cabin on Old Grange Road?

"Well, he did seem a little put out." As always, the doctor sounded calm and patient. "Donny's heart is in the right place, but he can be a reckless young man."

Reckless enough to attempt a kidnapping? "I wonder if I could talk with him," she said. "To apologize."

"He went out to breakfast at the café. What was it you needed, Susan? How can I help you?"

"It's about my son, Michael."

"I remember the day when Michael was born," Doc said. "Early spring, but the weather wasn't much different than what we've got today. A big snow coming in. You and Grant hadn't been here long. You were living in that temporary trailer near Pinedale."

A sob caught in her throat as she thought of that special day. Grant had been far more upset than she was, utterly panicked when she woke up in labor and informed him that there wasn't time to go to the hospital as they'd planned.

"Of course we have time," he'd said, phoning Rachel for a second opinion. "What about all those nurses? They told us you'd be in labor for hours and hours."

"They were wrong."

Then Susan had been wrenched by a labor pang so deep and fierce that she knew the delivery time was near. Every fiber in her body urged her to push.

When the pain had subsided, her husband had been near, holding her hand. "What am I supposed to do?" he'd asked. "Should I boil some water?"

"What for?"

"I don't know." His blue eyes had been wide and terrified. "In the movies, they always boil water. Maybe it's for tea."

Gathering her strength for the next assault of labor, she'd snapped, "I'm having a baby, Grant. I'm not in the mood for a beverage."

It was then that Rachel had come in the door of their tiny trailer. At a glance, she'd figured out what was happening. "It's time. I'll get my dad."

"I'll go!" Grant had shouted. He'd pulled on a sweatshirt. His thick brown hair had been flying in all directions.

"No," Rachel had said. "Susan needs you here."

Calm and beautiful as an angel, she'd kissed Susan on the cheek. "You'll be all right. This kind of miracle happens every day. I'll be right back."

Through the red-hot agony and wrenching pain, Grant had stayed with her. He'd supported her efforts. He'd coached her on the breathing techniques. And she knew he'd felt her pain.

Even after Doc arrived, he'd stuck by her.

After what seemed like an eternity of labor but was

really only a few hours, she'd turned to him. "It's okay if you take a break, honey."

"You need me," he'd said. "I'll always be here for you, Susan. Always."

She remembered the inexpressible tenderness in the way he'd held her, as well as the wonderment in his face when Michael had appeared with all his fingers and toes attached, mewling like a kitten.

To Doc, she said now, "I remember."

"An easy birth," he said. "All I had to do was stand by and catch. How old is Michael now?"

"Five. He'll be six in April."

"Is he ill?"

"Why would you think that?"

"I'm a doctor, Susan. Why else would you consult with me about your son?"

"Yes, of course."

She was losing it. Too many complicated deceptions tangled in her brain. She wanted to ask direct questions and receive truthful answers. She was too tired and too stressed; her supply of cleverness had been depleted.

"Susan? Was there something else you wanted to talk about?"

"Rachel." The name blurted from her lips. "I've been thinking about the fire a lot. It was such a terrible accident."

"Yes," he said. "An accident."

"Afterward, Grant and I were never the same."

"Let me tell you something I've learned from years of being a doctor," he said. "An unexpected death is hard on the people who are left behind. Some wounds never heal, but we've all got to go forward. We grieve. And we keep on going. To do otherwise would be to dishonor the memory of the dead.''

"What about revenge?'' she asked.

"That's an easy emotion, Susan. Forgiveness is a lot harder.''

Didn't she know that? To forgive…to forgive Grant…

"And mercy,'' said Doc. " 'The quality of mercy is not strained, It droppeth as the gentle rain from heaven.' ''

"Is that from the Bible?''

"Shakespeare, *The Merchant of Venice*. Are you all right, Susan?''

Someone else had quoted to them. O'Dell had said something about an eye for an eye and roses at her grave. Were the two connected? Kindly Doc Evanston and that nasty old alcoholic made extremely strange bedfellows. Thinking of them together was impossible.

"Susan?''

"I'm okay,'' she said. "Goodbye, Doc.''

She hung up the phone. More confused than ever, she tried to weigh forgiveness against revenge. She never thought of herself as a vengeful woman, but she still hadn't forgiven Grant.

After spending the day with him, she could see how much he'd changed. He was more like his old self. Maybe even better. All that counseling had helped. He was almost sensitive. As for loving him—she wasn't sure that her love for Grant had ever died.

The telephone shrilled, and the sound was like a scream. Her eyes flew to the clock. It couldn't be the kidnappers. Not yet. It wasn't time.

Breathless, she answered, "Hello?''

"Did you miss me, Susan?"

She recognized the shorter kidnapper's voice. "Where's Michael? Is he all right?"

"Now you know what it's like," he said. "Now you know what it means to miss someone, to live for the minute you'll see them. There's only one thing worse. Know what that is, Susan?"

"Please let me talk to Michael."

"I asked you a damn question. What's worse than missing someone you love?"

Was this a riddle? She didn't know what he was talking about. Her fingers trembled on the plastic telephone receiver. "I don't know," she said.

"To know that your loved one is never coming back."

Panic fluttered her pulse. "What are you telling me?"

"The truth. Did you get the money?"

She looked through the open door of Grant's office. The battered suitcase was still inside the safe. "Yes. I've done everything you asked."

"All four hundred and fifty thousand?"

"Every bit of it." Maybe she should have held out, given him something to worry about. But she couldn't control her fear enough to negotiate cleverly. "You've got to tell me. Where is my son? I need to talk to my son."

"That can be arranged."

She heard a sudden noise. The curtained French doors leading to the hallway opened, and the taller kidnapper stepped through. He still wore his red patterned ski mask. In his arms, he held Michael, who was squirming frantically. A wide piece of brown masking tape covered his mouth.

"Michael!"

"Hold it," said the voice on the phone. "Bring out the money, show it to my partner, and he'll let your kid go."

She dropped the phone. Her eyes saw nothing but Michael. He was safe. They were almost free.

Susan rounded the desk. Her heart banged against her rib cage as she approached her son. "It's all right, Michael," she said. "I'm here. You're going to be—"

"Stop!" said the big man.

Like hell she would.

"I told you to stop!" From inside his parka pocket, he produced a black semiautomatic pistol, which he aimed not at her but at Michael.

Halfway across the lobby, she halted. "Let him go," she said.

"Do what I say, Susan. So far, you've been real good. Now I want to see the money."

"It's in the safe. Grant has the combination." She looked toward the eyeholes in his ski mask. "Please, let me hold my son."

"You're sure that you've got the money?"

"Yes."

Though his aim with the gun did not waver, he released Michael. As soon as the boy's feet touched the floor, he raced toward her.

Susan held out her arms and gathered him to her breast. Nothing in her whole life had ever felt so good and complete. His small body was warm and safe. Finally safe!

With a quick yank, she pulled the tape off his mouth.

"Ouch!" he cried.

"Michael, are you all right? Honey, say something."

"I'm okay."

"My baby, I love you so much." She held him tight, and his little arms gripped her. Never again would she let him out of her sight.

"Hey, Susan," said the taller kidnapper. "We're not done yet. Go back to the phone."

Holding Michael's hand, she did as he said. "Hello?"

"What the hell is going on out there?"

"Don't worry. You'll get your money. It's locked in the safe and I don't have the combination. We have to wait for Grant."

"Yeah? Well, where is he?"

"Feeding the dogs."

Mentally, she tried to calculate how long it would take him to finish. His confrontation with the kidnappers would have to be handled carefully. If Grant came through the door and saw a man holding a gun on his son, there was no telling how he would react.

Over the telephone, the kidnapper said, "We'll wait. Put my partner on the line."

She held out the telephone receiver toward the other kidnapper. He had positioned himself at the end of the counter so he had a clear aim at them and at the front door. This man didn't seem cruel—not like his partner. But there was a directness about him that made her think he wasn't bluffing. "Your partner wants to talk to you," she said.

"Set down the phone. Come out from behind the desk where I can see you."

They changed positions. For the first time, Susan considered the possibility of escape. If she grabbed

Michael and ran toward the kitchen, they might be out of range of the kidnapper's gun. But she couldn't take the risk. Not now. Not when Michael was finally safe.

The big man hung up the telephone and came out to stand near them. He gestured with the gun, and she stepped back. "We'll do what you say," she assured him. "You won't hurt any of us, right?"

"Hey, we haven't hurt anybody. Mikey, did we hurt you?"

"No," he said in a tiny voice.

The front doorknob rattled. The man in the ski mask turned his pistol toward the sound. The door burst open and Snuffy bounded inside. The big golden retriever bounced past the kidnapper to Michael and snuggled her nose against him.

Grant came inside. In his parka, boots and hat, he looked huge—bigger than the kidnapper and ten times more dangerous.

"Hold it," the kidnapper said. He raised the barrel of his gun. "The safety's off, and I'm ready to fire."

"Please, Grant," Susan said. "Everything's fine. It's okay. They just want their money."

His face was red from the cold. He was breathing hard, as if he'd been running. "Michael," he said, "are you all right?"

"Yeah."

"Susan, is he hurt?"

"Please," she begged. "Don't do anything stupid."

"Stupid? You mean, like defending my son. My home." He stared coldly at the kidnapper. "What kind of man do you think I am?"

"A smart one. Let me tell you, buddy, if you try

anything, I won't shoot you first. First bullet is for
the kid. Then the woman.'' He gestured with the gun.
''Go over there and stand next to them.''

When he didn't move, the kidnapper said, ''Want
me to show you how this works? I can start off by
killing the dog.''

''No!'' Michael cried.

''All right,'' Grant said. He strode across the lobby
toward them, bent down to hug Michael, then picked
the boy up in his arms.

''You stay right there,'' the kidnapper said. ''All
three of you stay together until we get the money out
of the safe.''

''Yeah, sure,'' Grant said. ''No problem, buddy.''

He sounded strong, not at all frightened, and that
worried Susan. Hopefully Grant wasn't planning to
overpower this man with a gun.

''We're going to wait,'' said the big man.

''For what?'' Grant asked. ''Just take your money
and run.''

''Our getaway is all figured out.''

''By your partner? Is he a pretty smart guy?''

''Real smart. He wanted for me to tell you something, Grant.''

''Yeah?''

''He said: She's prettier than her picture.''

Grant looked toward the portrait of Susan, signed
in the corner with Johnny's trademark rose. O'Dell
had mentioned roses on a grave. The postmistress had
told him that the ''artist fellow'' lived on Old Grange
Road. Johnny Rosewood.

He was the other kidnapper—the brains of the two.

Johnny had easy access to Pinewood. While he was
in and out, working on Susan's portrait, he could have

gone through the papers in Grant's office, discovering the amount of the insurance payoff. He could have stopped by Pinewood at any time, could have seen the note on the calendar about Michael's arrival.

But why had Johnny turned kidnapper? He had no reason to hate Grant. It was hard to believe that the only motive for this crime was the ransom.

And why had Johnny instructed his partner to mention a clue that would reveal his identity? A chilling fear struck deep in Grant's heart. If they knew who Johnny was, could he leave them alive to testify against him?

Grant heard scuffling from the hallway behind the French doors and turned to watch as Johnny shoved Sven Dahlberg into the lobby.

"On your knees," he ordered Sven.

The tall blond developer obeyed without question. All the bluster had gone out of Sven. He said not a word.

Johnny's dark eyes glittered as he stared at Grant. "Thanks for the bonus. Sven might be useful."

"Why, Johnny? Why are you doing this?"

"You'll find out soon enough. First, let's take care of the money. It's in the safe. Right?"

Grant nodded.

"Get it for me, Grant." Johnny cocked his handgun and aimed the barrel at Sven's right ear. "If you try anything, my partner is going to shoot your kid. And I'll kill Mr. Dahlberg."

Bitterly, Sven said, "I'm afraid that's not much of a threat. Grant wouldn't care if you blew me away."

"That's where you're wrong," Johnny said confidently. "You see, Sven, it doesn't matter if he hates your guts. Guys like Grant like to think of themselves as rescuers, protectors of people who've gotten into trouble. Isn't that right, Grant?''

''Nobody has to get hurt.''

''But you messed up, didn't you? With Rachel. You didn't rescue her.'' His mouth curled in an ugly sneer. ''Get the money.''

Careful not to make sudden or threatening moves, Grant went into his office. The big man had stepped into the doorway to keep an eye on him, but his attention was divided, as he also watched Susan and Michael.

Grant twisted the combination lock. There were objects in here that he could use as weapons. The suitcase itself was heavy. If he flung it at the kidnapper...

Sven would die.

Gritting his teeth, Grant restrained his urge to fight back. It was his fault that Sven was here. Besides, he couldn't purposely cause the death of another human being. And he couldn't put Susan and Michael at risk.

He removed the suitcase and held it up so the kidnapper could see. ''What do you want me to do with it?''

''Bring it into the lobby.''

Stiffly, Grant obeyed.

''Put it on the floor,'' Johnny ordered, ''and open it.''

Grant squatted down. He was ready to spring at Johnny, to disarm him. But what about the other guy?

He flipped up the latches and showed them the stacks of money, all denominations.

''There you go, Cyrus,'' Johnny said to his partner. ''Didn't I tell you this would work? Half for you. Half for me.''

''You were right.'' The other man laughed as he

pulled off his ski mask, revealing a big, homely face. "We got the money. Smooth as silk."

"Rachel liked silk," Johnny said darkly. "She wore a silk blouse when I painted her."

His words trembled with a heat and a passion that was scary as hell. Had he been obsessed with Rachel? Though Grant couldn't imagine Rachel being unfaithful to Charley for this little weasel, it might have happened. Susan had often told him that there was nothing more irresistible to a woman than a man who adored her.

"Time for the getaway," said the one called Cyrus. "We need to make tracks before the snow gets too deep."

"Right." Johnny looked down at Sven. "We don't need you, do we? You're kind of a problem. Might be best if I shoot you. Just in the arm or the leg. That would keep you from running."

"Knock it off," Grant said.

Johnny laughed. "Always the hero. Right, Grant? You don't want me to hurt this guy in spite of all the stuff he's pulled on you."

"Sven's got money," Grant said. "You could ransom him."

"But who'd pay for him?" Johnny slapped at Sven's shoulder. "Get up. Go stand with them. We're going into the kitchen. You, too, Grant."

The four of them—the hostages—formed into a tight little group. As soon as Grant came close enough, he picked up Michael and carried him. To Sven, he said, "I'm sorry. I never expected this."

"Are they going to kill us?"

Each of them could identify the kidnappers. Johnny

and his partner, Cyrus, would be foolish to let them live. "I don't know."

"Of course not," Susan said to Sven. "They aren't going to assassinate four people. The one called Cyrus doesn't want to hurt anybody. Just do what they say."

"Shut up!" Johnny ordered.

"We'll cooperate," she promised. They had Michael back, and that was all she wanted. The money wasn't important.

As Johnny and Cyrus trailed behind them at a distance of about six paces, Susan clung to Grant's arm. Her gesture was more to hold him back than anything else. They would be all right. She had to believe they would be all right, that if they went along with the kidnappers, they would all survive.

"You were here last night," Grant said over his shoulder. "Which room?"

"Second floor, the last room in the back," Cyrus answered.

"What?" Susan said. "They were in the hotel last night?"

"That's right," Grant told her. "I found O'Dell's truck in the parking garage."

"This is a nice place," Cyrus said. "Real soundproof."

"I should have figured it out," Grant said, "when Randy told me Michael was watching Saturn Patrol videos. Nobody but me has Saturn Patrol."

"Mommy does," Michael said.

Susan smiled at her son and patted his arm. "I thought you were watching the videotape I packed in your suitcase."

"Other ones, too," he said.

"My videos," Grant said. He kept his voice calm, but she could feel the steely tension in his arm. "They took my videos from the television in the lobby. And they got food from the kitchen. Right, Johnny?"

"We had to eat."

Grant glanced toward Susan. "That's why you had to wipe crumbs off the countertops the first time you went into the kitchen. They'd been in there, raiding the refrigerator."

"Keep walking," Johnny ordered as they entered the kitchen. "Now, we're going to steal your truck to get out of town. I figured that out this morning. Why should we take O'Dell's old heap when we've got a choice?"

He directed them all the way to the far end of the kitchen. "Okay, this is far enough. Put down the kid, Grant. Then take your car keys out of your pocket. Real slow."

Susan prayed that Grant wouldn't make any sudden moves. Their only chance was to believe the kidnappers would do as they promised. They had their ransom. If Grant cooperated, they would drive away. Everything would be fine.

Grant took out his keys.

"Put them on the counter," Cyrus ordered.

"Why'd you do this?" Grant asked him.

"For my share of four hundred and fifty thousand. Heck, that's not a bad payoff for two days' work."

He reached out, grabbed the keys and pocketed them.

Gesturing with the gun, Johnny indicated the door that led to the basement wine cellar. "Sven and Grant, I want both of you to go in there and close the door so I can lock it."

Grant objected, "I want to stay with Susan and Michael."

"Too bad." Johnny aimed his pistol at Snuffy, who had followed them into the kitchen. "Don't make me shoot the mutt."

"Okay," Grant said. "We're going."

"You boys ought to be real comfy down there. I checked it last night and there's even a couple bottles of wine. You can pass the time getting drunk until somebody comes by to rescue you."

But Susan knew that Grant would be out of the cellar in two minutes. How could Johnny have missed noticing the dumbwaiter?

A dark feeling came over her. Johnny didn't intend to keep them alive. How could he? They knew his identity, and they could identify his partner from police mug shots.

She glanced toward the small, dark man. A weird intensity radiated from him like static electricity. She had the sense that he was toying with them, the way a cat plays with a mouse before the kill.

Why was he doing this? He didn't even know her, had no reason to want her dead.

Johnny turned to Grant and snapped, "Move it. Both of you go into the wine cellar. Now."

Grant pivoted and followed Sven down the stairway into the wine cellar. "Come on, Snuffy. You can stay here with me."

The door closed and Johnny motioned for Susan and Michael to step back while he fastened the door lock and the padlock.

"Okay, Susan," he said. "Now, we're going to go upstairs."

"Fine. We won't cause any trouble."

Holding Michael's hand, she left the kitchen and went through the lobby.

"Up the stairs," Johnny instructed. "Let's hurry it up."

She walked swiftly down the carpeted second-floor hallway. The room Johnny had chosen for them was at the far end of the west wing of Pinedale, the part that overlooked the river.

Before Johnny closed and locked the door, he said, "You won't get too lonely up here, Susan. I'll be back for you."

GRANT'S FIRST PLAN of escape from the wine cellar was to try the outer door where deliveries would be made. With Snuffy at his heels, he strode between rows of empty wooden shelving. The air in the cellar hung heavy with dank moisture. After Pinedale was open, the temperature in here would be regulated to a precise sixty-two degrees, but it was considerably colder now.

"What are you doing?" Sven demanded.

"Getting the hell out of here!" he shouted back.

Grant climbed the wide concrete stairway at a run. Though the door was equipped with a dead bolt to prevent theft of his liquor supplies, he seldom bothered securing the wine cellar. He yanked at the handle. Locked! Of course! Nothing could be easy.

Sven and Snuffy stood together, looking at him expectantly.

"It's locked," Grant said.

"Listen, Grant, it might be best to sit back and wait. I really don't think they're going to hurt us. They're just going to make their getaway."

"They have my wife and son."

"But maybe they'll just take the money and high-tail it out of here."

"And maybe not." Grant confronted him. "That's not a chance I'm prepared to take."

Beneath the dim light from a single bulb, he stared into Sven's face. The braggart was gone. Every trace of smug superiority had vanished from the tall blond man's countenance. It was as if Grant was seeing the real human being beneath Sven's thick facade.

Intense danger tended to strip away a person's outer shell. Often, Grant had seen this change in people during rescues, when their inmost fears were laid bare. Some crumbled. And some of the most unlikely people were heroes. Under the successful exterior, what kind of man was Sven Dahlberg?

"I'm not a coward," he said. "I know you don't have any reason to believe me, Grant, but I'll do whatever it takes to help."

"Why? If I was out of the way, you could take over Pinedale."

"I'm not a monster, Grant. Just a developer, looking out for his profit margin." His eyebrows pulled down in a scowl. "I don't want to see anything happen to the kid. What's the plan?"

"First, we've got to get out of this cellar." He strode toward the dumbwaiter. "Over here."

"By the way, your ex-wife is a hell of a woman. Most broads would be crying or screaming their heads off, but she's cool."

"Don't get any bright ideas about moving in on Susan."

"You're divorced," he said. "Tell you what, you can have Melanie. I'll take Susan."

"First you want my hotel. Then you want my ex-wife." Grant was only half joking. "As soon as you're away from the guy who's got a gun pointed at your head, you start making deals. What is it with you, Dahlberg?"

"You never know unless you try," he said. "Not that I really think I've got a chance with your ex. It's pretty damned obvious that she's still in love with you. Now, how do we get out of this basement?"

"The dumbwaiter."

Grant didn't bother with explanations. Now, finally, was the time for action.

After he'd tucked his large frame into the four-foot-square cube and promised to send it back down for Sven, he hesitated. This three-story dumbwaiter from cellar to ballroom was meant to be used for transporting wine and trays of food. It wasn't designed for lifting the weight of a grown man. Would the cables hold? Were the counterweights adequate?

He would soon find out. Using the pulley, he hoisted himself to the kitchen level, stopping when he was even with the door that should have slid up easily, except for one small obstacle. There was no latch on the inside. He pushed on the stainless-steel slats, tried to pry from the bottom. The door wouldn't budge.

"Damn."

From below, Snuffy made a sympathetic-sounding whimper.

Sven called up to him, "What's wrong?"

Grant tried the door again. It wouldn't move.

Cramped inside the dumbwaiter, he began to sweat. His shoulders bunched in a tight knot. Thank God he hadn't closed the back side of the dumbwaiter, or he would have been tightly enclosed in the cube.

He dug inside his pocket for his Swiss Army knife. Using the blade, he worked at the door. But the excellent craftsmanship thwarted him. Not even a sliver of space showed at the bottom of the door.

One floor up, at the ballroom level, the dumbwaiter door was wood—more decorative and less perfectly fitted.

He informed Sven. "Can't get the kitchen door to open. I'm going up to the third floor."

Aware of the minutes ticking away, he yanked on the pulleys, ascending the narrow shaft. The steel cables creaked, protesting his weight. At the second floor, the drop to the concrete basement floor was over forty feet, and he was trapped inside this box with no room to maneuver, no room to breathe.

For an instant, he considered turning back, trusting that Johnny and Cyrus wouldn't do anything more dangerous than take the money and run. But Grant didn't believe it. Johnny Rosewood was after something more than the ransom. He'd seen insanity in the artist's dark eyes, and he felt certain that Johnny never would have revealed his identity if revenge hadn't been part of his plan.

At the ballroom level, Grant manipulated the latch using his knife. He was out.

His lungs expanded. His senses were alert. The waiting, the helplessness, the not knowing had strained his nerves to the breaking point. This was better.

Quickly, he sent the dumbwaiter back down to the basement. From here he could operate the pulleys. Within a few minutes, Sven stood beside him in the serving area outside the ballroom.

"Now what?" Sven whispered.

"Let's make sure we don't run into them."

Outside the ballroom, Grant heard the sound of voices. They were coming down the hall from the guest rooms. Cyrus had said they'd spent the night in the second-floor far-west wing.

Taking a careful peek, Grant saw the two kidnappers descending the stairs. Susan and Michael weren't with them.

"But we've got to count the money," Cyrus was saying.

"Don't be stupid. That'll take forever."

"You're not going to cheat me, Johnny. Half of that money is mine."

Grant couldn't believe that these two idiots had outsmarted him. Holing up at Pinedale had been a stroke of genius. Last night, when he and Susan had danced in the ballroom, when she'd collapsed in tears, they'd been within a hundred yards of their son.

He turned to Sven. "Go to the end of the hall. There's a stairway. On the first floor, there's a mudroom with coats and boots. You can probably find something that fits."

"I'm on my way."

Before he left, Grant caught hold of his arm. "Thank you."

The blond man grinned. "It never hurts to do favors for a friend."

IN THE FRONT LOBBY, Johnny glared as Cyrus popped open the latches on the suitcase and started pawing through the currency.

Johnny wasn't interested in the ransom. He hadn't done this for the money. It was for Rachel.

For a minute, he savored his revenge. Grant had

been helpless against him. The great rescuer had stood by, like a pathetic fool, while Johnny had given the orders.

And the best was yet to come.

As soon as he got Cyrus out of the way, Johnny would bring Grant and Susan together for the final time. He hadn't exactly decided how he would kill her. A fire would be poetic justice. Susan should die in a fire. Just like Rachel.

Johnny's best inspirations always came at the end of a painting, when the sketches were done and only the final strokes of a brush were needed to bring his portrait to life—or to death.

Chapter Ten

Susan perched on the edge of the bed, holding Michael's hand and talking gently to him. She tried to hold her fears at bay, but Johnny's words kept repeating in the back of her mind. What had he meant when he'd said he would be back for her?

Why? This ordeal was supposed to be over. She'd done everything they said. Paid them the ransom. Obeyed their orders. They should have been safe. Instead they were captives of a madman. Her thoughts turned toward methods of escape. They had to get away from here. Johnny wouldn't let them live. Not now when they knew his identity. She would feel a lot better once they were gone from Pinedale, far away from Johnny Rosewood and Cyrus.

"Michael, you don't still have my cell phone, do you?"

"Nope. Johnny took it."

Worried, she stroked the dark brown hair off his forehead. "Do you want to tell me, sweetheart? Tell me about Johnny and Cyrus."

"I don't remember, Mommy. I was sleepy."

Later, she feared, the memories would come back to him, but she would be ready for that traumatic time. She would work through this horrifying experience with him. "You've been very brave. Soon, we'll be with your father."

"They gave me shots in my butt."

He scowled and his blue eyes—just like his father's—were angry.

"Then what happened?"

"I saw a new Saturn Patrol video."

"Want to tell me about it?"

"Yep. It all started with the red planet...." His words tumbled over each other as he recounted every detail of the video he'd watched.

Susan listened with one ear, keeping alert for signals of danger with the other—the approach of footsteps outside, whispering, gunfire.

Longingly, she glanced toward the door. In most hotels, it was impossible to lock a guest inside their own room, but Pinedale had old-fashioned, solid-oak doors with glass knobs and quaint-looking keys that locked, like a dead bolt, on either side. She and Grant had decided from the beginning that they would preserve as many of the original fixtures and designs as possible. They hadn't really expected for anyone to be purposely imprisoned in their room.

"And the green guy whacked the dragon."

Michael went silent, and she turned to him. "Then what happened?"

"I missed part of it. Cyrus was watching with me and he said his ski mask was itchy. So he took it off. And Johnny got really, really mad at him. I don't like Johnny."

"Me, neither," Susan said. "Why was Johnny so angry?"

"Because I knew how they looked." He rolled his

eyes. "Then Cyrus said, 'No. Nobody would believe a kid.' That's not right. Is it, Mommy?"

"You should always tell the truth about things that happen to you," she said. "I'll always believe you, Michael."

"Good people believe kids. And bad people don't. Right?"

"Kind of."

There was a tapping at the door. "Susan, it's me."

She ran to the door. Her fingertips pressed hard against the smooth, oak surface. "Grant, can you get us out of here?"

"I can't get to the keys. Johnny and Cyrus are in the lobby. Is Michael okay?"

"I'm here, Daddy."

"Good boy," he said. "Susan, go to the window and open it. You'll be able to climb down from there. I'll bring ropes and help you. Wait for me."

Climb down from the window? In the snow? "Isn't there any other way? Can't you break down this door or something?"

"I don't want to make noise. I don't know how long they'll be here."

"All right," she said. "Hurry."

Johnny's threat echoed in her ears. He would be back. For her.

Somehow, she had to stop him. There had to be something she could do. She looked around the nicely furnished room with two full-size beds with carved, cherrywood headboards and a matching nightstand. Was there something in here she could use as a weapon?

Bad idea, she decided. Johnny and Cyrus had guns. They probably wouldn't stand still while she tried to clunk them with a lamp. Then her eyes lit upon the dresser. If she couldn't get out, it might be wise to arrange things so they couldn't get in.

"Okay, Michael. We're going to make this room into a fort. Help me push the dresser."

The tall, six-drawer dresser was a big heavy piece. Like the headboards and nightstand, it was part of the original furniture at Pinedale. As Susan dragged aside the area rug and pushed, the hardwood floors were gouged. It took all her strength to move the solid wooden dresser. Her injured ribs ached as she strained every muscle.

Finally, they were done.

"There," Michael said.

"There, indeed."

The dresser stood flat against the door. It would take some effort for Johnny to get past the obstacle.

As Grant had instructed, she went to the window, opened it, detached the storm window and stuck her head out. The snow-swept view was spectacular. Below them, the Rampart River swelled to the edges of its banks where ice spread, attempting to contain the churning black waters.

They were going to climb down there?

A tiny ledge, no more than two-feet wide, separated the hotel from the cliff leading down to the river. Susan guessed that the drop from the window to the ledge was thirty feet. From there to the heavy, snow-covered boulders at the river's edge was another twenty.

A dangerous descent, but not impossible—especially if Grant was helping. When it came to mountaineering skills, she trusted him implicitly. Just last night, he'd helped her up and over the boulders when they'd gone to search the cabin on the Old Grange Road.

She looked down again. If they could find solid footing on the ledge, they could inch along, hugging the wall. The distance to the west end of the building didn't appear to be far at all. Leaning out into the falling snow, she saw a forest. If they could hide among the trees, it was possible they could escape.

She had no parka, but all of Michael's things were in the room. "You'll need to bundle up, son. Do you have your jacket and mittens?"

"How come?"

"Like your dad said, we're going to climb out the window and escape." This plan sounded like something the Saturn Patrol might attempt. "I want to be sure those men can't take you away from me again. Never again."

Michael looked out the window, then turned back to her. He shook his head. "Safety first, Mommy."

His comment was so typically Michael that she had to laugh. This was the boy who always made sure their seat belts were fastened and that they looked both ways before crossing the street, even when the light was green. She loved this little person with all her heart. "You're a smart kid, Mike."

He stepped back a pace. His eyes narrowed.

"What's wrong?" she asked.

"You called me Mike," he said. "You never call me Mike."

"You don't mind, do you?"

"I like it." His small shoulders straightened, and he stood as tall as he could. "Mike is a big-kid name. From now on, I'm Mike."

"Does that mean you're not my little boy anymore?"

"Yeah, I am."

For an instant, she saw a flicker of panic in his eyes. Like his father, he was doing a fine job of covering up his fear and behaving like a hero. "I'm so glad you're smart, Mike. And I need for you to be tough. Just for a little while longer. Okay?"

"Okay."

She looked out the window again. The snow was falling steadily in big, wet, cottony flakes. She pushed the window almost closed so they wouldn't freeze, and turned to Michael.

In order to make this climb, they needed rope, and Grant had said he would return with the necessary equipment. But what if he was delayed? She wanted out of there and, unfortunately, Pinedale didn't come equipped with pitons and other climbing gear in every room.

"We might as well do something," she said to Michael.

"Can I still call you Mommy?"

"Always. I'll always be your mommy." She stripped the sheets off the bed and tore down the long curtains at the window. "Help me, Mike. We're going to make a rope."

With her son's well-meaning but not-very-efficient assistance, Susan started tying together the sheets and curtains into a long, thick strand. She strolled around the room while she worked and then stood beside the window. Outside, the snow swirled. She could barely see across the river to the other side.

Climbing down would be perilous, especially for her. She could tie a harness around Michael and lower him, but she would have to climb. And Susan wasn't an extreme rock climber. If she fell, it could mean disaster.

Maybe this whole escape was unnecessary. Maybe Johnny had just been trying to scare her when he said he would be back.

If Grant used one ounce of common sense, he would lie back and wait until the kidnappers had driven off in his truck. Then he could come up here and let them out. They would be fine. They could call the state patrol and let the police do their job in catching the kidnappers.

But she'd seen the ferocious expression on Grant's face when they were held at gunpoint. She'd heard the implicit threat in his voice and knew that he'd ended his brief sojourn into sensitivity.

With a sigh, she realized that she could never force her ex-husband to change. And, to be perfectly honest, she wasn't sure that she wanted him to be different. Today might be a fine time for Grant to exercise his macho tendencies. She and Michael could use a hero right now.

NO MORE MR. NICE GUY. No more sensitivity. Patience had gotten Grant nowhere. He knew what he needed to do, and he didn't give a damn if Susan considered his behavior to be rash and arrogant.

First, he would make sure Susan and Michael were safe.

Then he would go after Carolyn's ransom money.

Grant raced down the hallway to the opposite side of Pinedale and met up with Sven near the door. He was wearing a parka he'd found in the mudroom.

"What next?" Sven asked.

"I say we get the hell out of here."

"I'm with you."

Together, they went outside. The snow fell thick and heavy. The temperature had to be subzero. This wasn't a blizzard, but it was close.

Running, Grant led Sven to the dog enclosure. Though the pack had taken cover inside their heated shelter, they bounded out to greet him.

"Hey, Grant," Sven said. "I like your mutts as much as the next guy, but this isn't the time to be playing around."

"Here's what we do," Grant explained. "I'm going to hitch up the team to the dogsled, go around to the other side of the hotel and get Michael and Susan."

"What about me?"

"The sled won't have any speed if the dogs are pulling the weight of three adults." He looked Sven in the eye. There was no reason to trust this guy. The opposite, in fact. "You can take off running right now or you can help."

"I'll stick." His gaze didn't waver. "When Johnny had a gun to my head, you kept him from pulling the trigger. I owe you."

"I want you to create a diversion so Johnny won't notice what's going on at the back of the hotel. Use my truck, then drive on into town."

"Wait a minute. Didn't they take your keys?"

"There's a spare key under the bumper on the driver's side." Grant had always told Susan to keep a spare key, and he was careful to take his own advice.

Sven brushed a coating of new snow from his

shoulders. "You think the truck will start? It was pretty cold last night."

"I already had it going this morning. It started."

In minutes, Grant had hitched a full team of eight to his lightweight dogsled. Always ready. He was always prepared to respond to rescue calls at a moment's notice.

In harness, the unruly bunch of tail-waggers took on a professional demeanor. They were as alert as he was. The dogs were ready to run, responsive to his every command.

Sven was tromping through the new snow toward the end of the building.

Grant ran behind the dogsled, not putting his weight aboard. He needed to save the dogs for later. At the corner of the hotel, he signaled to Sven. "Now! Go now!"

On the dogsled, Grant swung wide of the hotel at the very edge of the parking lot. Unless Johnny was standing at the window watching for him, he wouldn't notice.

His dog team responded like the champions they were, pulling the sled with ease. He stood behind the sled and the dog bag, guiding Amble, the lead dog, with voice commands. "Let's go. Now."

Though the parking lot was covered in four inches of new snow, it was glare ice underneath, and they flew across the surface.

His timing couldn't have been better. Just as Grant came even with the front entry to Pinedale, he saw Sven feeling under the bumper for the spare key. With any luck, Johnny would be distracted by the truck pulling away. He wouldn't notice Grant, wouldn't think of Susan and Michael.

But what if Grant was wrong? Second thoughts flashed through his head. He could flag down Sven and stop right now. Wait until Johnny and Cyrus were gone. Free Susan and Michael. Later, they would notify the proper officials. He knew that Susan would have voted for that plan. She would prefer caution. She would tell him to be sensible, to forget the money, to be glad that none of them was hurt.

Yeah? And what would Grant get for being such a good boy?

He'd hesitated once before. At the fire. And Rachel had died. Grant wouldn't make that mistake a second time. He knew how to perform a rescue. Those volunteer missions had prepared him to make quick decisions and to act upon them. Already moving at full speed, he wouldn't hold back until he was one-hundred-percent sure his loved ones were out of harm's way.

At the far-west end of Pinedale, he guided the dogsled to a stop. "Whoa, Amble. Whoa." Hidden by the edge of the building, Grant watched as Sven fired up the truck.

In spite of the cold, the engine caught on the first try. The truck was reliable, and Grant had been prepared for snow and subzero temperatures. His truck always started.

Sven revved the engine twice before pulling away. "Careful," Grant whispered. The parking lot was sheer ice, and Sven hadn't taken time to clear off the windshield, except for a few swipes with the wiper that didn't remove the icy crust. He was driving blind.

As Grant had expected, Johnny heard the truck. He charged out the door from the lobby, aimed his gun and fired.

But Sven was already a good distance away—too far away for a handgun to be accurate. Somehow, with almost no vision through the windshield, Sven managed to make it out of the lot. The approach to the highway was a winding road, three quarters of a mile. Once Sven got to the main road, he would be safe.

Over the storm, Johnny shouted, "Big mistake! You won't get away from me."

The hell he wouldn't. Sven was driving like a champion, putting more and more distance between himself and the bullets. He was going to make it.

Cyrus burst out the door, running like a linebacker and firing his semiautomatic weapon wildly. He emptied the clip, paused and snapped in another. In spite of the drifting snow and ice, the big man was moving through the storm at a good pace. He overtook Johnny and kept on running.

"Come on, Sven," Grant urged. "You can do it."

If Grant had been driving, he could have made better speed. He knew every inch of this road. But Sven had only visited twice. He didn't know where he was going. He misjudged the last turn before the highway.

Through the heavily falling snow, Grant saw the black truck slide off the road into the banked snow.

Johnny and Cyrus were going after him, guns in hand.

Grant glanced over his shoulder to the rear of the hotel where Susan and Michael were locked in their room, waiting for his rescue.

But he couldn't leave Sven to Johnny's mercies.

"Ha, go!" Grant ordered the dogs.

He stayed at the edge of the forest, away from the road. The sled glided swiftly across the packed snow under the trees. Already, half a foot of new powder had accumulated in the field between the forest and the road. The snowfall swept around him, crusting on his eyebrows, stinging his face. It clung to the coats of his dogs, even as they ran.

Grant made the turn, heading toward the truck.

Johnny stopped dead still and stared in his direction. He yelled something unintelligible to Cyrus. The sharp report of two handguns made it sound like a war zone.

But Grant kept going. When he reached the truck, Cyrus was still plowing toward them, almost within range to get off a decent shot.

"Whoa!" Grant ordered the dogs. He waved to Sven with a gloved hand. "Get on!"

Sven dived through the snow toward the sled and climbed on.

"Stay down!" Grant yelled.

The weight of Sven's body would make it hard going for the dogs. If he went into the heavy snow of the field, they would make an easier target on their way back to pick up Susan and Michael. Even if Johnny didn't hit them, he would know Grant's intention was to return to the hotel.

In a split-second decision, Grant kept his dog team on the road—a faster, icier surface. At first the dogs were slipping, struggling for traction. Then they got the sled moving. Grant ran behind the dog bag, holding the bundle. Within ten yards they were charging fast, heading directly toward Cyrus. He urged the dogs forward, "Hike, hike."

"What are you doing?" Sven yelled.

"We need a gun." If he was going to have a

chance to rescue Susan and Michael, they needed to be armed.

"You're crazy!"

They were bearing down on Cyrus. The big man was far ahead of his partner on the road. When he saw the dogs coming straight at him, he froze.

The worst thing that could happen would be that Cyrus would shoot one of the dogs. The sled would slow down. They might all be killed.

"Cyrus!" Grant yelled, focusing the big man's attention on him. "I'm here! Come on, shoot me!"

Too late, Cyrus raised his arm and took aim.

The lead dog veered only slightly, and the two huskies running at point and swing positions banged into Cyrus. He went down with a thud. It was a bad fall, heavy and clumsy. And Cyrus dropped his gun.

"Get it!" Grant yelled to Sven. "Get his gun."

From his position on the sled, Sven leaned out and scooped up the semiautomatic pistol.

"Don't shoot," Grant told him. A clip only held fourteen bullets, and they didn't have any more ammunition. "We've got to make every bullet count."

Johnny had realized what Grant was doing. He was stumbling back toward Pinedale. Every few steps, he turned and fired.

Grant wouldn't risk his dogs again. Now that they were armed, some of the pressure was off. He took the longer way through the field, directing the dogsled toward the west end of Pinedale.

He left the sled at the edge of the hotel and told Sven, "Pick your shots. Make each one count."

"Where are you going?"

"To get Susan and Michael."

Running, Grant circled the hotel. He stepped onto

the ledge above the river and looked up toward the room where Susan and Michael were held captive. "What the hell?"

A pathetic rope, made of sheets and curtains tied together, dangled from the window. Packed on his sled, in case of emergency, Grant had state-of-the-art climbing gear. But there wasn't time for rigging.

"Susan!"

Her head poked out from the window. "What's going on?"

"They're shooting."

"Get Michael out of here!" she shouted. "I'll lower him."

"You can't use that flimsy rope."

"Shut up, Grant."

He heard gunshots from behind him. Sven or Johnny? One bullet, then two. How many had already been fired?

"Grant!" Sven yelled. "Johnny is almost to the front door. I can't get off a good shot from here."

Once inside, it would be only a matter of minutes before Johnny reached Susan and Michael.

Grant called up to Susan. "Let's do it."

"We're ready!" she yelled.

Hand over hand, she pulled the rope back inside. It was just long enough.

She'd made a harness for Michael and tied it securely beneath his arms. Susan had spent enough time working with mountain rescues to know the proper knots, even if she was using bedsheets.

His eyes wide and excited, Michael climbed onto the window ledge. She hugged him one last time. "You're going to be okay."

"I love you, Mommy."

"And I love you. A hundred times a bazillion."

From below, she heard Grant urging. "Come on, son. It's just like the rock climbing we've done."

Except that Michael wasn't wearing standard safety gear. And it was snowing heavily. The wind lashed against the rear of the hotel as Susan lowered her son from the window. In seconds, she was wet from exposure to the heavily falling flakes.

Grant had eased himself along the narrow, precarious ledge and stood directly below Michael. The drop was thirty feet from the window, but it seemed like a lot less with Grant's outstretched arms reaching up. She could barely stand to look down. If they fell from there, it was another twenty to the weathered boulders at the river's edge.

They had to make it. Her arms strained with Michael's weight. Carefully, she let him down. Lower and lower.

From behind her, she heard the key being turned in the lock. The door banged against the heavy dresser she and Michael had shoved into place as a blockade.

"Let me in!" Johnny roared. "Susan, you can't get away from me."

As she watched, Grant grabbed hold of Michael and held the boy's small body against his own.

The rope went slack in her hands. Thank God! Michael would be safe.

On the ledge, there was virtually no room for maneuvering, but Grant managed to unfasten the makeshift harness. He looked up at her. "Anchor the rope and climb down."

"It won't hold me. Go! Get Michael out of here."

"I'll catch you. Come on."

They needed to get off that damn ledge.

Looking toward the door, she saw the dresser moving as Johnny pushed, cursing under his breath. The space was six inches wide and growing larger as he battered the oak door. If he got inside, he could come to the window. He could shoot her son.

She looked down at Grant. He held Michael against his chest. Silently, his eyes beseeched her.

This was the final time she would say goodbye to him. "I forgive you, Grant."

"What?"

"I've always loved you."

Deliberately, she released the end of the rope and watched as it slithered over the ledge and fell to the river's edge.

She slammed the window shut. She staggered back until her knees encountered the bed and she sat on the bare mattress. She slowly turned her head until she faced the hotel-room door.

Johnny's rage crashed around her. He screamed hoarsely as he battered at the door. The crack widened. In a few minutes, he would be in here.

She should have been frightened, but the intensity of the last twenty-four hours had been too much for her. Inside, she felt drained, empty.

"Let me in!" Johnny shouted.

In a soft voice, she said, "You're too late."

Apparently, he'd heard her because the hammering stopped. He was quiet. Then he said, "Susan."

"You're too late, Johnny. Michael's gone. You can't hurt him anymore."

With a sustained final effort, he pried open a space wide enough for him to squeeze into the room. He, too, was wet from being out in the snow. His black hair was plastered down on his forehead. His complexion was sallow, and he looked dirty. Cold and dirty.

He rubbed his hands together for warmth, and she noticed his long artistic fingers. He reached into his belt and took his gun.

"I never cared about Michael," he said. "You're the one I wanted."

IN THE PINEDALE BALLROOM, Susan sat quietly on the bench beside the player piano. The curtains remained closed, creating an artificial night, though it was only eleven o'clock in the morning. The chandeliers and sconces were lit.

Johnny paced back and forth on the parquet floor with a gun in each hand. "He'll come back for you," he said. "And when he does, I'm going to be ready for him."

Cyrus slumped on the floor beside the doorway. Beside him was the battered suitcase containing her mother's four hundred and fifty thousand dollars. The big man groaned, rubbing at his knee. "I think I busted something, Johnny. We got to get out of here."

"I don't need your whining."

"We can take O'Dell's truck and go."

"No. We're staying right here." Johnny pointed to the floor with the barrel of his gun. "There needs to be two of us. If I was here by myself, Grant might think he could overpower me. But with two of us, he knows that even if he shoots one, the other could kill Susan."

"I don't want to kill anybody."

"That's not what it looked like when you ran out the door and chased the truck."

"I was mad," Cyrus said. "I don't think so good when I get mad."

"It's okay, Cyrus. As far as I'm concerned, things couldn't be better."

Confusion was written in the creases and lines of Cyrus's big, flat face. "Couldn't be better? What do you mean?"

"More money, Cyrus. We can get more ransom." He gestured toward her. "We have a hostage."

"I don't get it," Cyrus said.

Johnny squatted down in front of him. "Here's how it works. Pretty soon, there's going to be cops outside, but they won't come in here because they'll be scared that they might hurt the lady. Then, they contact us on the telephone, and we make demands."

"Like what?"

"A helicopter." Johnny leaned close to his partner. "And more money."

Cyrus gaped. "You think the cops are going to give us those things?"

"Oh, yeah." He nodded as he rose to his feet. "Not only that, but we're going to be famous."

Johnny Rosewood grinned as he strode across the ballroom to the curtains and looked out at the falling snow. He hadn't planned it like this, but he was glad that everything had turned out the way it did. Fate had finally acknowledged him.

Hostage situations were always a big deal on the news. Pretty soon, there would be television crews outside. They would show his name. They would tell his story. If the reporters were smart, they would even show his paintings on national television. He would become an instant celebrity.

"I hope the weather clears up," he said. "I want those reporters to get through."

"You're wrong," Susan said. "If I were the queen of England, the media might get excited. But why would people be excited about me being held hostage?"

"Think about it," he said. "Newspeople love this stuff. A crazed artist. A lovely woman. The mother of a five-year-old boy. Holed up in a big, deserted hotel in the mountains. Not to mention your heroic ex-husband, who's done all those rescues."

"But I'm a nobody."

"Not to Grant," he said. "Even if nobody else gives a damn, he'll be back here to rescue you."

"Grant and I are divorced," she said. "We had a terrible custody battle over Michael. He has every reason to hate me. He'll be glad to have me out of the picture."

"Out of the picture?" Johnny chuckled. "When I'm painting, especially a portrait, that's what I think of. What's out of the picture. What's not included in the physical view, and how I can manifest those invisible qualities. When I painted your portrait, I talked to Grant. A lot."

He probably knew Grant better than she did. "He told me you were a good mother to Michael. Patient and always honest about what you told him."

He studied her. Very symmetrical features. Her ebony-black hair made an exquisite frame for the pale oval of her face. In the portrait he'd done of her, which was done from a photograph, he hadn't really captured the luminescent glow of her skin and the faint blush of her cheeks.

Johnny continued, "Grant loved to hear your

laughter. He said the sound was pure and that it cleansed him.''

Her eyes misted.

''Oh, yes,'' Johnny said. ''And he liked to watch you cook. He said that when you moved around the kitchen, you were like a magician.''

As Johnny watched, her expression subtly transformed. Her edge of fear was still there, but she was feeling something else. He knew that look. He could tell that she was a woman deeply in love.

He averted his gaze, not wanting to feel sympathy for her. ''He loves you, Susan. He loves your voice, your face, your manner, everything about you.''

''You're mistaken,'' she said.

''Grant's love is what makes my revenge so perfect. He loves you, but he'll never have you again. For the rest of his life, he'll be tortured by your memory, by the fantasy of what might have been. Dreams are so much more powerful than reality, don't you think?''

''I don't know.''

''If Grant had been living with you, day by day, he would notice the annoying little things you do. Like not hanging up your clothes. Clearing your throat too often. Waking him up when you're restless in bed. But he's forgotten. In his memory, you're perfect.''

Like Rachel. He couldn't recall a single detail about her that wasn't pleasing. ''When I was painting Rachel's portrait, she—''

''Johnny,'' Cyrus whined. ''My knee is swelling up. I need a doctor.''

Johnny raised the gun in his right hand and aimed it at the big, stupid oaf. ''Maybe I should shoot you and put you out of your misery. Like a crippled horse.''

"It hurts."

"But there needs to be two of us. Do you have the gun?"

Cyrus raised his handgun.

"Remember, partner, if anybody comes through that door, you aim it at her and pull the trigger."

Johnny heard a sound from outside the closed door to the ballroom. It was time. Grant Richardson, the big hero, was coming back for his wife.

Chapter Eleven

"Is that you, Grant?" Johnny shouted.

Catlike and quick, he moved closer to Susan. The cold bore of his gun pressed against her temple. Surely Grant wouldn't be foolish enough to come back here. Even if he did have feelings for her, he wouldn't give himself up as a hostage.

"Don't try anything," Johnny warned. "I've got a gun to her head."

Silence, punctuated by the screaming wind outside, settled over them. Without moving her head, Susan said, "You were wrong. He's not coming back. Nobody's out there."

"He's there. I can feel him."

His hand was trembling. The gun barrel bumped her, just above her ear, and Susan recoiled. What would it be like to be shot? Killed instantly? Would she feel any pain?

"Show yourself," Johnny said loudly. "Tell you what, Grant. If you don't show yourself right now, I'm going to shoot a bullet through her right hand."

He grabbed her wrist, and she gasped.

"Cyrus is still here," Johnny shouted. "So don't

think about running in here and rushing me. If I miss, my partner will kill her.''

There was another pause. Another long silence. Johnny forced her hand down flat on the piano bench.

She wanted to be brave, to endure the pain without flinching. If Grant was outside the door, she didn't want to do anything that might cause him to come in here. But Susan wasn't a hero.

Johnny held her wrist. Her fingers splayed against the black piano bench. His gun pointed at the tensed veins in the back of her hand. She imagined the bullet as it pierced skin, flesh and bone. ''No,'' she cried. ''No, don't.''

''You've got three seconds, Grant.''

''Stop!'' she shouted. ''Can't you understand? He's not out there. Nobody's there. Don't do this.''

''One... Two...''

''All right, Johnny. You win.''

The sound of Grant's steady, deep voice filled her with relief. He hadn't abandoned her. He'd come back.

''Open the door,'' Johnny ordered, ''and slide your weapons in here. Take off your parka and throw that in here, too.''

The door opened a crack. Two handguns skidded across the floor. Grant's parka followed.

''Now, walk inside,'' Johnny said. ''Real slow, with your hands up over your head. Close the door behind you.''

Logically, Susan didn't want him to come through that door. She didn't want for Grant also to be captured. But when she saw him, tall and strong, with his hands over his head, her heart began to beat again, and her blood flowed a little warmer. She felt hope.

Grant kicked the door shut behind him. Though he was the hostage, his strong, masculine presence was overpowering. "Let her go," he said.

Johnny released Susan's hand, but kept the gun trained on her. "Frisk him, Cyrus. He might have another weapon."

Groaning, the big man limped over to Grant. He searched the pockets of Grant's wool plaid shirt, patted down his jeans and pulled out a wallet. Being thorough, he even ran his finger around the edge of Grant's boots. "He's clean."

"There's a cell phone in the pocket of my parka," Grant said. "Somebody wants to talk to you, Johnny."

He beamed with insane delight. "And who might that be? Sheriff Walt Perkins?"

"Pick it up," Grant said. "The line is already open."

"Here's how this works," Johnny told him. "Cyrus and me have both got our weapons trained on Susan. If you make any sudden moves, if you try anything fancy, we're going to shoot her."

"I won't try anything."

Johnny's ash-white face brightened. His thin lips curled in a smile that was pure evil. "Too bad you missed our little chat. Earlier, I was telling Susan how much you loved her. That's true, isn't it? You love the way she laughs, the way her black hair falls across her high cheekbones."

Though Grant did not acknowledge the words or the emotion, his eyes showed his yearning. For her? Was it really true? She wanted to believe every mocking word Johnny said.

Darkly, Johnny continued, "That's right, Grant. I

want you to love her. Because it's going to hurt worse when she's gone."

"You're sick," Grant said.

"Here's an idea," Johnny said. "Why don't you two stand next to each other? You can get to know each other again, and I can keep an eye on both of you at the same time. Come here, Grant."

When he crossed the parquet ballroom in long-legged strides, she couldn't hold back any longer. With a cry, she ran to him. Her arms circled his body, and when he embraced her, she collapsed against him. Though the situation was impossible, she knew he would take care of her. She knew it.

"Where's Michael?" she whispered.

"He's with the regular person who baby-sits for me. He's fine."

Johnny was on the cell phone and they listened to his end of the conversation. "Is this Walt Perkins? Yeah? Well, here's a news flash for you, Sheriff. Me and my partner have got guns aimed at Grant and Susan. If there are any of your men inside this building, we'll shoot these two hostages. And Walt? This is the last time I'm talking to you. You'd better get somebody more important on the phone."

He clicked the cell phone closed and looked at Grant. "Is there anybody else in the building?"

"Not as far as I know."

"Who's out front?"

"The sheriff and five deputies."

"Has he called for backup?" Johnny asked.

"Walt contacted the Colorado State Patrol. Sven is working on the FBI. Within the hour, they'll be all over this place."

"Good," Johnny said.

Grant's arms tightened around her. His body was so broad and strong that she felt shielded. They had to get out of this alive. They needed to have a future. After years of anger and frustration, they had something to live for. They could be a family again.

"Let's go," Johnny said. "We're going down to the office, so we can get some direct telephone communication with people who are important."

Cautiously, they descended the main stairway into the lobby. All the while, Johnny shouted out their intentions, warning off anyone else who might try to stop him.

When they reached the lobby, Cyrus limped to the windows and peeked outside. "There's three cop cars, all right. Lights are flashing. But it's snowing pretty hard. I don't see anybody moving around."

In Grant's office, Johnny took the authority position, standing behind the desk. "The office makes a good command post. No windows. Only one door. Everybody get comfortable. We're going to be here for a while."

Susan huddled on the sofa beside Grant, holding his arm. The physical contact reassured her.

Cyrus settled on a chair opposite them. Moaning, he propped his foot on another chair and arranged his leg.

"You've got some swelling around your knee," Grant said.

"It's killing me."

"I can help." Grant nodded toward the closet. "Over there. I've got first-aid stuff."

"No," Johnny said. "Don't listen to him, Cyrus. It's a trick."

"I don't care, man. I gotta do something. This hurts."

"All right, you big baby."

Johnny went to the closet, found the emergency medical supplies in two neatly labeled cases. He dropped them on the floor beside Cyrus. "Remember, Grant. Don't try anything. I'll kill her."

"You've made that real clear."

As Grant went to work on Cyrus, binding his knee with Ace bandages, Susan kept her eye on Johnny. Though his gun still pointed at her, his gaze focused on Grant. There was such deep loathing in his coal-black eyes. How could an artist who was capable of creating beauty be so caught up in ugliness? There had to be something more true and honest inside him. Maybe she could reach out, convince him that vengeance was foolish. Maybe she could talk him into letting them go.

She cleared her throat and his eyes returned to her. Quietly, she asked, "Why, Johnny? Why do you hate Grant so much?"

"He killed the woman I loved."

"Rachel," she said. "But she was married to Charley Beacham."

"He was eight years older than she was. Too old for a vibrant woman like Rachel."

He settled down behind the desk, resting his gun hand on the desktop, keeping his aim steady.

"She started coming to my cabin in the autumn, to sit for a portrait that she planned to give to Charley. The first time she came, we walked through the trees and talked about her picture. She was so beautiful. Her hair was like a flame—russet, amber and scarlet—against the golden aspen leaves. She seemed to glow. Like a goddess.''

His expression softened as he remembered. Even his voice sounded different. ''Every time she came to pose for me, she brought a rose. I always sign my paintings with a rose. Nobody else had ever been that thoughtful.''

Rachel had been good with gestures. She'd always known the right words to say, the appropriate gift for every occasion. But she wasn't perfect. If Susan recalled correctly, Rachel was someone who made a wonderful acquaintance, but she wasn't much of a friend. Her charm was as ephemeral as smoke, without weight or substance.

''After I finished her portrait,'' he said, ''I wanted to keep it. So I asked her to come back for another. And she did. She liked having me paint her picture. Once a week, almost every week, she came to me. I was doing the best work of my life. We fell in love, made love. Damn, it was wonderful. We even talked about how she could divorce Charley and live with me.''

He frowned. ''An artist doesn't make much money. I really couldn't afford to support her, but we were working it out. And then, there was the fire at Pinedale.''

''The accident,'' Susan said.

''That's what I thought at first.'' His jaw tightened. ''Do you know where I live?''

''I haven't seen your house,'' she replied. ''But I know it's up on Old Grange Road.''

''Rachel's father has a couple of rental cabins up there,'' Johnny said. ''A couple of weeks after the fire, I saw him, sitting in front of one of the cabins.

It was vacant at the time. I didn't know Doc very well, but I was desperate for contact with anyone who had been close to Rachel. Do you know what he told me?"

Susan shook her head. "I don't."

"He explained about the explosion that started the fire, said that Grant should have known better, should have checked all those propane canisters. And when it started, Grant could have gotten to Rachel. That's what Doc said. He told me that Grant could have saved her."

Johnny's head whipped around on the stem of his neck. His dark eyes bored into Grant's broad back and shoulders. "That's right! You were careless. You caused the fire. And you didn't save her. Doc had you pegged. He hates your guts. Almost as much as I do."

Johnny looked angry enough to shoot Grant right on the spot, and Susan tried to divert his attention. "Doc was upset. It was right after the tragedy. I'm sure that after he had the chance to think about it, he changed his mind."

"It wasn't the only time I talked to him," Johnny said. "He came back to the vacant rental cabin. I waited for him. We talked a lot. I showed him my pictures of Rachel, and he bought the original portrait from me."

"I talked to Doc Evanston earlier today," Susan said. "He told me that vengeance dishonors the memory of the dead. 'The quality of mercy is not—'"

"Shut up, Susan. I've heard that speech, and I don't buy it."

She tried another direction. "Rachel was a good person. She wouldn't want you to hurt anyone else."

"She was my muse," he said. "After she died, all

the color went out of my world. I haven't done any-thing good since she died. Except for your portrait.''

"The one in the lobby," Susan said.

"I was dead broke," Johnny explained. "I needed work, and I knew Grant was hiring. So I came here to Pinedale. The minute I stepped through the door, I could feel Rachel's presence. Like the place was haunted."

"Don't talk about that," Cyrus interrupted. "I don't like ghosts, you know what I mean? I didn't even want to stay here last night."

Johnny exhaled an exasperated sigh. "It turned out okay, didn't it?"

"Yeah," Cyrus said. "I didn't see any ghosts."

"There are supposed to be some," Susan inter-jected. "When we first bought this place, people told us all kinds of scary stories. I guess every old hotel is supposed to have ghosts."

She liked to believe that the Pinedale ghosts were benevolent spirits who approved of the renovations. A lot of people, like Adrian Walker, remembered Pinedale with fondness. She prayed those ghosts would help her now.

Turning back to Johnny, she said, "If you came up here to work as a laborer, how did you end up paint-ing my portrait?"

"Somebody told Grant I was an artist, and he asked me."

And this was how Grant's kindness was repaid—with a kidnapping and hostage situation. So much for random acts of kindness.

Johnny continued, "There was something about the portrait, something about working with Grant that in-spired me, made me feel alive. I had to complete the cycle. An eye for an eye. After my vengeance is complete, I can be whole again."

"So you blame Grant for—"

"For everything," Johnny concluded. "And I will have my revenge."

She couldn't bear thinking about his insane ideas for revenge, especially since she was the most likely target. "It's wrong, Johnny. Everything you're thinking and doing is backward."

"I don't need your approval."

She looked toward his partner. The big man might be able to be convinced. He might change his mind. "What about you, Cyrus?"

"Ma'am?"

"You know this is wrong, don't you? When Johnny hooked up with you, he didn't tell you that anyone was going to die."

"No, ma'am, he didn't."

"You don't want to kill me," she said.

"I'm not a murderer," Cyrus declared. "That time in Abilene, I didn't mean for the guy to be dead."

Oh my God, he was a killer, too. But Susan wouldn't allow herself to completely despair. In a rush, she offered, "Cyrus, if you give up right now and return the money, we won't press charges. You'd get off with a light sentence."

"Shut up!" Johnny came around the desk and stood over her. "Not one more word."

Grant was between them. Behind Johnny's back, she could see him considering a move. Their eyes met, and he shook his head. Not yet. Not while Johnny stood over her with a gun.

"I dunno," Cyrus said. "It's not a bad deal, Johnny."

"Do it my way and you can keep this money and a whole lot more," he promised. "She's trying to play you for a fool, Cyrus. Don't listen to her."

His big shoulders slumped. "I dunno."

Though none of them spoke and there were no windows to let in the noise from outside, the room wasn't silent. Susan heard the sounds of four people, each enduring their own brand of stress. Johnny fidgeted, tormented by his unquenchable vengeance. Cyrus, still in pain in spite of the first aid, breathed heavily. Her senses were attuned to Grant on a special, high-frequency level, and she could hear the steady hum of his energy, like the low growl of a cougar preparing for the hunt. And from herself? Her breath kept catching in her throat in a whimper that only she could hear.

She'd tried talking to Johnny, drawing him out. But she'd only succeeded in making him angrier.

When the telephone on the desk rang, they all jumped.

Johnny grabbed it. Into the receiver, he said, "This had better not be Walt Perkins."

He listened for a moment, then nodded. Satisfied. "Wait," he said. "I want my partner to hear this."

Still aiming his gun at Susan, he said to Grant, "Put this on the speaker."

Grant flipped a few buttons. "It's on speakerphone."

"Sit over there with Susan," he ordered.

Johnny directed his voice toward the phone. "Could you repeat that? Who's this?"

Over the speakerphone, a deep male voice came through, loud and clear. "This is Special Agent Kevin Wilson, FBI, and I'm calling from Denver."

"Denver?"

"We can't get up there. It's snowing like hell down here."

"I don't believe you," Johnny said. "You're not coming up here because you don't think I'm important."

"You're mistaken, sir. We take all hostage situations seriously."

"Unless you get yourself up here, I'm done talking to you, mister."

He disconnected the call. "I want news teams. I want coverage."

"I don't like this," Cyrus said.

"Shut up! Let me think!"

Distracted, Johnny had dropped his guard. On the sofa beside her, Susan could feel Grant's body tense. He was preparing to attack.

Just then, Johnny swiveled, raising his gun again. "Don't try it. Don't make a move."

"Be reasonable," Grant said. "If you let us go right now, you won't be in much trouble."

"You could get help," Susan added.

"Psychiatric help?" he asked with a sneer. "I'm not crazy. Not a bit. I'm going to get out of here. I'll need a helicopter and another five hundred thousand dollars. And I'm going to get it."

"Cyrus." Susan turned to the big man. "You don't want to go to jail, do you?"

A shot rang out. Her ears reverberated with the blast. She gasped and stared wide-eyed at Johnny.

"That was a warning, Susan. You'd better shut up. Both of you. In fact, I'm going to get you out of the way so I can make my arrangements. On your feet."

"Where are we going?" Grant asked.

"Not far. Only into the safe."

"You can't put us in there," Grant observed. "You don't know the combination, and we aren't much good as hostages if you can't get to us."

"Then I guess you'll have to tell me how to open it." The telephone on the desk was ringing again, but Johnny ignored it. "Open the door, and I'll write the numbers down."

Grant hesitated. "We could suffocate in there."

"Then I guess you'll have to tell me the combination."

RANDY GAYLOR WAS surprised when Sven Dahlberg strolled into the offices of Slade's Adventures, waved to his mother and greeted him. "Could I talk to you for a minute, Randy?"

"Sure." He'd never thought Sven noticed his existence. Maybe he wanted to show him something about the plane.

Though Randy had been sticking close to the Mountain Rescue phone, making up all kinds of excuses so his mother wouldn't be worried, he followed Sven outside. On the porch, they still had a bit of shelter from the storm.

Sven didn't waste any time. "I have a message for you, Randy. From Grant."

Randy blinked slowly. This was too weird. Sven and Grant were total enemies. "You do?"

"Grant wanted me to tell you that Michael is okay. He's staying with that woman who baby-sits for him. And Grant asked me to give you this."

Sven held out a Saturn Patrol wristwatch.

"Michael's favorite. The Saturn Patrol." Randy felt a hundred times better inside. Michael had been rescued, and he—Randy—had helped. "Can I tell my mom?"

"Not yet, but don't worry." Sven patted him on the shoulder. "There are a few details, but I'm taking care of it."

THE DOOR OF THE SAFE clicked shut and the black darkness of an airtight tomb surrounded them. The total absence of light disoriented Susan. It was as if she'd suddenly been struck blind, and her other senses needed to compensate for the loss. She whispered, "Grant?"

When he caught hold of her and pulled her close, she felt his presence with heightened awareness. His wool shirt rubbed against her cheek. She felt the strength of his muscles, the tautness of his torso.

Gently he stroked her hair and murmured, "I'm sorry, Susan. God, I'm so sorry."

"You're forgiven. For everything." She tilted her head up toward him. "Kiss me."

In the darkness, his mouth found hers. The sweet pressure of his kiss awakened sensations she'd never expected to feel again. She was melting, yet tense. There was a trembling in the pit of her stomach, and she moaned with pleasure.

He broke away. "Are you all right?"

"More, Grant. Kiss me again."

His tongue moistened the surface of her lips, teasing lightly. His passion was both familiar and brand-new. Like their love. It could never be as it once was. The past was gone. And yet, she loved him more completely at this moment than ever before.

He deepened the kiss. Gently, beautifully, his touch consumed her. His fingertips lightly traced her spine, brushed against her rib cage. When he cupped her breast, she felt the stirrings of arousal. And she offered herself freely, without the slightest reservation. She wanted his touch to last forever. In his arms, she was transported to another world, a better place, a place where they could be happy.

"My darling Susan, I've missed you so much."

"Don't stop."

"We have to talk," he said.

"Why?" She wanted to forget about everything that was going on outside the door. If only for a moment, she wanted to believe in the future, their future together.

"I'm turning on the light," he said.

Though he didn't release her, she could feel him stretching, groping overhead in the darkness.

The glow from a forty-watt bulb seemed like an intense spotlight after the total darkness. She squinted up at him. "I don't suppose there's any way to get out of here."

"None."

Inside, the safe was no bigger than a standard walk-in closet. The ceiling was low, only seven feet. The walls were plain, painted white and lined on one side with metal shelves and numbered lockboxes. Across the back wall was a rack for hanging furs. "How much air do we have in here?"

"I don't know. I suppose there's enough for a couple of hours, if we don't do any heavy breathing."

Suffocation would be a horrible way to die. She didn't want to consider that particular possibility. Instead, she focused on Grant. With her fingertip, she traced the line of his jaw. "Why did you come back for me?"

He smiled down at her. His eyes had never seemed so blue. "You know me, Susan. I always have to be the hero."

"Really, Grant. Why?"

"Because I love you, darling, with all my soul. I'd walk into hell for you."

She sighed. "Let's hope that's not where we are. In hell."

"Not hot enough," he said.

With a contented smile, she relaxed in his arms, resting her head against his chest. Being close to him felt so wonderful. Never again would she leave him. Never.

"I have a plan," he said.

"Somehow, I knew you would. What is it?"

"I worked this out with Sven before I came back here. He'll coordinate the phone communications into the hotel, making sure—sooner or later—that Johnny has to allow someone from the outside to come in here and see us."

"A check on the hostages?"

"Right. And whoever comes in here will be bringing two guns. One for himself. One for me."

"What good will that do?"

"The logistical problem is that there are two of them. Even if I could take one of them out, the other could shoot."

"So you figure that if you even the odds, you can win."

"Something like that."

It didn't really sound like much of a plan to her, but she was willing to try anything. "What should I do?"

"When you see me start to make my move, get out of the way. Get down and don't look up."

"All right."

He eyed her suspiciously. "You're not going to argue with me?"

"I trust you."

"You do?"

"I'm looking at it this way. Negotiations with Johnny are impossible. He's crazy." She snuggled against him. "It's time for a hero."

"You know how much I care about you, don't you?"

"I'm beginning to," she said. "What did you think of Johnny's story? Sad, wasn't it?"

"Not really. Do you think Doc Evanston hates me that much?"

"I really did speak with him this morning, Grant. When you were out with the dogs." Right before the phone call from Johnny, when they went from the frying pan into the fire. "Doc talked about mercy and forgiveness."

"If he has to forgive me, he thinks I did something wrong."

She hadn't thought of Doc's comment in that light. He wouldn't forgive Grant if he'd thought the fire was an accident. It wasn't fair. Grant was the last person on earth to be negligent. If anything, he was annoyingly well-prepared for everything. "I don't get it," she said. "Doc seems to be such a sensible man."

"He has a blind spot where Rachel's death is concerned. You understand, don't you? If anything happened to Michael—"

"It won't," she said vehemently. "Don't talk about that, Grant. It came too close."

"There was another thing I didn't like about Johnny's sad story," Grant said. "I kept thinking of Charley. He was her husband, and she was playing around with this little weasel. No matter how he wants to make it sound romantic, they were having an affair behind her husband's back."

Johnny's unrequited love wasn't quite so pretty when viewed from that perspective. "Very true."

"And let's get real, Susan. There's no way Rachel would have married a destitute artist."

"No way at all," Susan agreed. Grant's assessment was cold, cynical and absolutely accurate. "Johnny was just a diversion that got out of hand."

She might have pitied him, but his supposed love had turned into a dark and horrible specter that had threatened her family. He couldn't have been in love. Not really. True love could never be repaid with vengeance.

"We might as well get comfortable in here." He took off his wool shirt and laid it on the cold, tile floor. "Care to sit down?"

The interior of a locked safe was a long way from candlelight and roses, but she thought his gesture was incredibly romantic. "Thank you."

She settled on his shirt, and Grant sat beside her with his arm draped around her shoulders. She snuggled against him, and when she looked up, he kissed her again.

Tugging, she pulled out the tail of his turtleneck from his jeans. Her hand slid underneath the soft cotton fabric and she stroked his chest. She'd always loved the crisp texture of his dark hair, his muscular body, his maleness.

He nuzzled her ear. "I wish we knew what Johnny

was doing out there. If I knew for sure that he wouldn't come charging in here at any minute, I'd make love to you, Susan.''

"Right here? On the cold hard floor?"

"You're not really shocked," he said.

"Not at all." She felt the same way. "We'll get out of this, Grant. We'll have a whole lifetime to make love."

"You've always been the optimist," he said.

She kissed him, slowly, savoring the taste of him. "And you've always been my hero."

Chapter Twelve

"Finally," Johnny said into the speakerphone. "You sound like somebody I can deal with. What television channel do you work for?"

"Channel Five in Denver."

Johnny leaned back in the desk chair. Things were going his way. He knew that if he bided his time and waited, the right moment would come. This TV newsman, Frank Cavell, had been up at Silver Mountain, skiing. When he'd checked in with his office, they'd told him about the hostage situation. The newsman had gone to Walt Perkins outside Pinedale, and now Walt had put him through.

"Here's what I want," Johnny said. "I'll release the hostages in exchange for a helicopter and five hundred thousand dollars. And I want it in an hour."

"You got it, Johnny."

He could hardly believe his luck. "An hour, right?"

"I think I can work it out. There's only one thing. How do I know the hostages are still okay?"

"They're fine," Johnny said tersely.

"I need to see for myself. Can I come in and see for myself?"

"What's the deal, Frank? This sounds like a trap or something."

"Well, you caught me, Johnny."

He chuckled. This guy had a real pleasant voice, professional-like. Though Johnny didn't watch any television, he could easily imagine a guy like Frank being a newsperson.

"Caught you?"

"I was hoping I could get an interview with your hostages. With all of you."

An interview on television? For a moment, Johnny considered, then decided he didn't want to share the limelight with Grant and Susan. "If you want an interview, I know who you can talk to. Doc Evanston. He lives in town. You tell Sheriff Perkins to bring Doc up here."

"Fair enough."

"Call me back when the chopper is here."

Johnny switched off the speakerphone. It was a smooth deal. Easy. Maybe too easy.

Cyrus mumbled, "I don't like it."

"Let me do the thinking."

"You've never been in jail, but I have. I don't want to go back there. Not for the rest of my life."

"Nobody's going to jail," Johnny said. They would have a helicopter. The pilot could take them anywhere and drop them off.

"We should give back the money," Cyrus said. "Nobody gets hurt. And we get a minimum sentence."

"You're a moron. Know that?" He'd been carrying this big, stupid oaf throughout the whole kidnapping and hostage situation. "We're getting everything we want. We'll be rich."

"If that chopper isn't here in forty-five minutes, I'm turning myself in."

"It'll be here."

What reason would a newsman have to lie? Frank Cavell was going to get exclusive rights to Johnny's story. He would tell everybody about how Johnny had loved Rachel, and he would show the paintings on television.

Everything was working out fine.

GRANT HELD HER in the circle of his arms as they sat together, leaning against the back wall of the safe. He kissed the top of her head and inhaled the clean fragrance of her shining black hair. Being with her was wonderful, and he tried to stay within this moment, this respite. He didn't want to think about the danger that lay just beyond the safe door.

"What's wrong, Grant?"

For starters, they were locked in a safe where they might suffocate. And then, just outside the door, there was a madman with a gun who had sworn to kill her. Not only that, but the sketchy plan he and Sven had come up with had as much chance for failure as success. "What's wrong?"

She nodded.

"You're amazing, Susan. Aren't you at all worried?"

"I'm terrified," she said. "But there's nothing I can do about it right now."

She'd always been good at taking things as they came. Bring on the disappointment and disaster, Susan could handle it.

On the other hand, Grant's talent was thinking ahead. In his mind, he tried to visualize the tactics they would need to overcome Johnny. But it was impossible to plan. There were too many variables. Which room would they be in? Where would Johnny be looking? What would Cyrus be doing?

Only one thing was certain: Grant needed another gunman and a weapon for himself to be sure he could overtake both Johnny and Cyrus. Two against two.

He sighed. "Why didn't I pick up on how crazy Johnny was when he was painting your picture?"

"I don't know."

"I enjoyed talking to him," Grant said. "He'd sit there and paint, and I'd go on and on about how beautiful you are and how much I missed you. In a way, it was better for me than the psychologists I went to."

"Why?"

"The counselors kept trying to help me accept the reality that you were gone." And he hadn't wanted that. He hadn't wanted to face the prospect of living out his life without Susan. "When I talked with Johnny, I could pretend we were getting back together. I'd stare at the portrait of you and imagine that you were coming right back, like you were just at the market, buying groceries."

"And all that time," she said, "he was plotting his vengeance and seeing Rachel's ghost."

"Crazy," Grant said.

His arm curled around her back. With his hand, he could feel the swell of her breast. As soon as this was over, he promised himself that he would carry her to his bed and make love to her. The flavor of their kisses lingered on his lips and made him hungry for more. "I'm starving," he said.

"When we get out, I promise to make you a ten-course dinner. With a T-bone and mushrooms. A potato soufflé. And those chunky brownies that you like.''

''You're a damn good cook,'' he said.

''A master chef.''

He kissed her ear. ''Actually, that wasn't the kind of hunger I was thinking about.''

''Me neither.''

Her eyelids slowly lifted. One brow arched, and her lips pouted in the sexiest grin he'd ever seen in his life. Oh, yeah, they were on the same wavelength.

''I haven't been with another woman,'' he said. ''Not since you left.''

''I haven't slept with anyone else, either.''

That pleased him. Of course, he hadn't expected for her to be celibate any more than he thought he would go two years without sex. ''So, you must be as horny as I am.''

''At least as horny.''

He wanted to cover her body with caresses, to bring her pleasure in a hundred ways. ''You know, Susan, I'm kind of an old-fashioned guy. There's something that feels weird about having sex and not being married.''

''You and I went to bed together before we were married,'' she reminded.

''That was different. It was before I knew how marriage could be.''

''I know what you mean. I missed you. I missed waking up in the morning, knowing that you'd be there beside me.''

Abruptly, he took his arm out from behind her and let her shoulders rest against the wall. Maneuvering around in the narrow space, he faced her and went down on one knee. He took her right hand in both of his and looked into her eyes, her lovely hazel eyes that sparkled with a slight green shimmer that always reminded him of springtime.

"Susan Falcone Richardson," he said, "will you marry me?"

She lifted his hands to her lips. "When?"

"Now." He needed no further time to think. He'd never been so sure of anything in his life. "Will you?"

"Yes."

He laced his fingers with hers and pulled her upright. They stood, facing each other. "I guess we should do some kind of ceremony."

"We've already had one," she said. "I wore my Italian grandmama's lace veil. You wore a tux. Somebody from my side of the family was crying."

"Your father," he said.

"Well, we don't need a ceremony like that again. Especially since my father wants to cater with refried beans."

But he wanted to say something to seal this agreement. There was so much inside him that he wanted to give to her. Grant cleared his throat.

"Susan, I promise to always love you and to honor you. In every way, I'll encourage you, support your dreams and give you the freedom to fly."

Her eyes misted with unshed tears.

In a soft voice she responded, "And I promise to believe in you, whether you're renovating a hotel or climbing Everest. I will respect you and love you. In sickness and in health. Forever and ever."

"Until death do us part."

From behind his back, Grant heard noises outside the door of the safe. Someone was working the combination. The heavy door opened, and Cyrus stood outside.

"I'm going to take your offer," he said. "I'll give back the money and let you go if—"

His words were cut short by a gunshot. His face contorted in pain. As his eyes squeezed shut, he stumbled backward, then sank to the floor in a heap. The back of his shirt was covered in blood.

"My God!" Susan cried out. "He's dead."

"I had to shoot him." Johnny stepped around the big man's body. "He was messing up."

"No," she sobbed. "You didn't have to kill him."

"It was easier than I thought. Now you know. I can kill somebody." He gestured with the gun. "Get out here. Slow and easy. No fast moves, Grant. I'll kill her, too."

Grant could see that Johnny was spooked, jumpy. His tenuous grasp on reality was slipping. He was even more dangerous now than before. His eyes darted nervously. His forehead was waxen with sweat.

"Now!" Johnny yelled.

Cautiously, Grant moved out of the unlocked safe. He turned toward Susan, who stood rooted inside. With terror-struck eyes, she stared down at Cyrus, who twitched slightly.

"He isn't dead." She looked at Grant. "Isn't there something you can do for him?"

"Leave him!" Johnny roared. "Grant, you go stand behind the desk. Put your back against the wall."

Though he wasn't sure what Johnny was trying to stage, Grant knew better than to ask questions. This scary little man was at the end of his tether, operating on nerves and misplaced bravado. It would only take one false step to set him off.

Johnny gripped Susan's arm above the elbow and dragged her forward until she was standing opposite the desk, facing Grant.

"There," Johnny said. "You stand right there."

He placed a battered bouquet of paper flowers in her hand and stepped back to study her, as if she were a painting, a work of art that he had created. He adjusted her arms, then tilted her chin upward so the overhead light shone on her cheekbones.

"Very pretty," he said.

The telephone on the desk rang and Johnny hit the button for the speaker. "What is it, now?"

"We heard a shot in there. What happened?"

"A gun went off," Johnny said.

"What about your hostages? Are they all right?"

"Tell me about my helicopter. Your time is up."

"Hey, Johnny, you gave me an hour, and it's only been forty-five minutes."

"Where is it?"

"The pilot is only about ten minutes away from here." The voice hesitated. "I've got to see the hostages before I turn over the money and the helicopter. Will you let me come in?"

Grant scowled to hide his excitement as he listened to this conversation. Though he didn't recognize the voice on the speakerphone, he knew the plan was still in effect, still on track. Somebody out there with Sheriff Perkins was negotiating with Johnny, and it sounded like they were close to an agreement.

If Johnny wanted any chance at a getaway, he would have to let this person come inside. And when he did, that person would bring a weapon for Grant and another for himself.

Without Cyrus, Johnny was at an even greater disadvantage.

The crude plan might work. Grant and Susan might be able to walk away from this disaster unharmed.

"I'll get back to you," Johnny said into the speaker.

Again he focused his attention on Susan, tidying her hair and straightening the bouquet in her hands. What the hell was all that supposed to be? "What kind of flowers are those?"

"Roses for Rosewood. And forget-me-nots." He laughed harshly. "Not much chance of that, huh? You'll never forget me."

Grant tried to gauge his chances for an attack. Still too risky. Though Cyrus was out of the way, Johnny still had his gun.

While he worked on her, like a mad sculptor with human clay, juggling his gun from one hand to the other, he talked in a low, tense voice.

"Poetic justice. That would be a pretty thing. A fire to kill the woman Grant loved. But there isn't time. No time at all. I have to improvise."

He moved away from her and nodded, satisfied. "Like a bride, a beautiful bride. Rachel would have been my bride. She would've carried roses. The flowers are a nice touch. Very nice."

He raised his arm straight. His gun aimed for Susan's heart.

"No," Grant said. "You don't hate her, Johnny. You want *me* to die. You hate me."

"If I kill you, Grant, it only hurts for a minute. If

she dies, you'll hurt for the rest of your life. Just the way I hurt.''

A single shot echoed in the office.

Johnny grabbed at his left shoulder and screamed. "Cyrus! Why aren't you dead? You're supposed to be dead!''

Grant started to move, to take advantage. But Johnny recovered too quickly. His gun was up again, pointing from Grant to Susan, who had ducked down on the floor.

As Cyrus struggled to brace his hand for another shot, Johnny aimed and pumped two more bullets into his former partner. Cyrus stiffened, then went completely still.

Johnny's shoulder was covered in his own red blood. He grasped at the wound, wildly waving his gun around. "It hurts. Damn, this hurts.''

Grant knew that the wound was painful but not lethal.

Aiming again at Susan, Johnny ordered, "Stand up, Susan.''

When she did, he jabbed the gun into her ribs and turned toward Grant. "You go over by the door to the lobby, Grant. Face the door.''

His instructions were poorly thought out, careless. The pain and tension had caused him to make a mistake. This might be the break Grant had been waiting for. When he crossed the office and stood at the door, he was only four feet away from Cyrus's body—and the gun Cyrus held in his lifeless hand.

The trick was to get the gun without setting Johnny off, without letting him know. Grant's first impulse, his heroic impulse, was to make a dive for the gun and shoot it out. But he couldn't take that risk. Not with Susan so vulnerable.

Johnny leaned across the desk. He picked up the telephone receiver and dialed. "Okay, I want you to send somebody in here to see the hostages. Hold on."

His breathing was labored. "Grant…"

"I can help you, Johnny. I can make it stop hurting."

"Shut up and listen. You're going to open the door and step into the lobby. If anybody's out there, you tell me. And if you lie, she's dead. If you make a run for it, you're signing her death warrant. Got it?"

"How do I know you won't kill her anyway?"

"You don't."

But he didn't have any other choice. As long as they were alive, there was a chance.

Grant opened the door to the lobby. Before he had returned to the hotel, he'd told Sven to keep everybody else back. The last thing Grant had wanted was a hail of bullets from well-meaning but clumsy rescuers from the Rampart Sheriff's department.

Apparently, Sven had managed to do as Grant requested. The lobby was empty. Through the windows, he could see the snow falling. The red and blue reflector lights of the police vehicles flashed steadily.

He shouted back to Johnny, "There's nobody here."

"Okay, Susan," Johnny said. "You're my shield. Stand in the doorway. And don't get any ideas about running. It's my left arm that's hurt, not my gun hand."

"I won't run," she said.

She was too petrified to even think about running. Her legs felt spindly and as fragile as spun glass. She jolted toward the door, taking care to avoid bumping Cyrus's body. Big, stupid Cyrus wouldn't have to worry about figuring things out anymore. Johnny had shot him dead.

Susan had never before seen a person die. Death came so suddenly, without ceremony. One moment, Cyrus had been breathing and speaking. The next, he was gone.

Behind her, she heard Johnny on the phone, but couldn't hear what he was saying. Her brain was whirling. She felt dizzy, faint. In front of her, she saw Grant.

"Be strong," he whispered. "It's almost over."

"Am I going to die?"

"He's going to let that guy come in here. He'll be armed. I'll be armed. We can take Johnny."

She didn't want to die, didn't want to be sacrificed to Johnny's revenge. There was so much to live for.

Forcing herself to inhale, she drew on her waning strength. How much longer could she endure this tension? When, oh, when would this be over?

From behind her, she heard Johnny hang up the telephone. Though she wasn't aware that he'd approached, the barrel of his gun poked into the small of her back.

"Somebody's coming in here," he said. "Until then, we wait."

Johnny positioned himself, leaning against the registration desk, with Susan standing directly in front of him. Grant was beside the front door, looking out.

"What do you see?" Johnny asked Grant.

"One of the police cars pulled away. The siren's going."

"Anything else?"

"The snow is still coming down, but it's slower now."

The storm had not yet become a full-fledged blizzard that would paralyze the roads and make travel impossible. To people who lived in the mountains, this kind of snow was a warning. Stay inside, stay warm and safe. The worst is yet to come.

The real blizzard for Susan was within her mind. It had started yesterday when Michael was torn from her. In the twenty-four hours since then, she'd suffered a fierce storm; a lifetime of devastation and hope. She'd found pleasure with Grant, their restatement of love and marital promises. And she'd experienced an intense fear, a horror that sank to the marrow of her bones.

"Someone's coming," Grant said.

She craned her neck. Soon, an armed man would come through the door. Soon, the terror would be over.

Through the front windows, she saw the shape of a man, bulky in his winter parka and hat. Susan prayed he would be a one-man SWAT team.

Without ceremony, the door opened and he came inside, stamping his feet and shaking the snow off his shoulders.

"Don't shoot," he said. The voice was familiar.

He pulled off his cap. "Now, Johnny, what the heck is going on here?"

It was Doc Evanston.

Susan's hands flew up to cover her mouth and hold back her scream. Doc Evanston! He was the one man in Rampart who hated Grant as much as Johnny did.

That was why Johnny had been whispering on the

telephone. He'd negotiated for Doc to come into Pine-dale.

"You've got to help me, Doc," Johnny said. "I've been shot."

"They told me you had a partner. Where's your partner?"

"Dead," Grant said.

"Are you sure about that?"

"Johnny shot him three times," Grant explained. "The first shot was in the back."

Doc sighed heavily. His complexion was ruddy from skiing the day before. He rubbed his hand through his thick gray hair and brushed at his walrus mustache. His pale blue eyes were unreadable as he picked up his black bag and came toward the registration desk. "What am I going to do about you, Johnny?"

"You've got to help me. I did this for you, too, Doc. It's revenge. For Rachel."

"Now, how am I going to fix your arm when you're holding a gun on Susan? And you've got another gun stuck in your belt."

"It's my left arm that got wounded. Come around here and work on it. Hurry, Doc. The pain is something awful."

Bending down, Doc set his black bag on the floor and opened it. "You're going to have to take off your shirt, Johnny, so I can see the wound and make sure the bullet is out."

"Okay. Take the gun out of my belt and keep Susan covered. Don't let up, even for a minute. You know what I'm talking about, don't you, Doc? You know that we have to get revenge on Grant."

Susan couldn't believe Doc Evanston would aim a

gun at her. He was a man of healing. He had attended at the birth of her son. And yet, that was exactly what he did.

Doc took Johnny's gun and pointed it at her. He turned his head to face her, and looked her in the eye. Then he winked.

"I'm awfully sorry, Susan. But you know how I feel. You know what Shakespeare said in *The Merchant of Venice*."

Mercy, she remembered. The quality of mercy.

Johnny was momentarily distracted as he struggled with his shirt.

Three things happened in such quick succession that they seemed simultaneous. Doc Evanston kicked his black bag across the hardwood floor toward Grant. Then Doc charged toward Susan, knocking her to the ground. She caught a glimpse of Grant, flying across the lobby like a hawk swooping down on his prey.

Doc was on top of her, covering her with his body. When he rolled off, she saw Grant holding a gun to Johnny's throat.

"Drop it," Grant snarled.

Johnny whimpered, then. His long, artistic fingers opened and his pistol fell to the floor with a thud.

It was over.

THAT NIGHT, IN THEIR private apartment in Pinedale, Susan hung up the telephone after talking with her mother, reassuring her for the tenth time that they were all right and that her savings were intact.

Amazingly, there had been no press coverage of the kidnapping and hostage taking. The supposed newsman, Frank Cavell, was actually a state trooper.

And everyone had followed Sven's directive for no publicity.

Grant had wanted it that way. After several widely publicized rescues, he'd seen firsthand how publicity could turn a situation into a dangerous circus.

Besides, everyone was focused on the weather, on the blizzard that was yet to come.

Contented, she strolled through the apartment that had been designed to her specifications. It would be wonderful to live here. She went into Michael's bedroom where Grant was tucking their son into bed. Snuffy lay across the bottom of the bed, keeping very still so they wouldn't notice her and put her outside.

Susan smiled down at her son. "Are you sure you can sleep with Snuffy in here?"

"Snuffy is my dog blanket."

Michael could barely keep his eyes open. Doc Evanston—the hero of the day—had checked him out and said that he'd been injected with a light sedative. The lingering effects might be a few more days of drowsiness, but nothing more dangerous.

Grant bent down and kissed his son's forehead. "What would you say if your mom and me got married?"

"I'd like it."

"Well, that's what is going to happen, Michael."

"Call me Mike. It's a big-kid name." He rolled over, eyelids already closed. "Night, night, don't let the bedbugs bite."

Susan whispered, "I love you, Mike. A hundred times a bazillion."

She and Grant crept out of their son's room and closed the door. When his arms wrapped around her, she said, "And I love you, too."

"You know, Susan, we got stopped before our wedding ceremony was finished."

"We did?"

"Right at the best part." He scooped her feet off the floor and carried her across the threshold into their bedroom, where he gently placed her on the bed.

Susan frowned up at him. "I thought our ceremony was perfect. We were honest, sincere, sensitive—"

"Can't forget 'sensitive,'" he said.

"What did we leave out?"

He stretched out beside her. "What do they always say at the end of a wedding ceremony?"

"I now pronounce you man and wife," she repeated from memory. Then she knew what was missing. "You may kiss the bride."

And so he did.

While the winter winds howled outside, they were warm and happy, safe from the threatening storm.

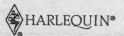

Take 4 bestselling love stories FREE

Plus get a FREE surprise gift!

Special Limited-time Offer

Mail to Harlequin Reader Service®

3010 Walden Avenue
P.O. Box 1867
Buffalo, N.Y. 14240-1867

YES! Please send me 4 free Harlequin Intrigue® novels and my free surprise gift. Then send me 4 brand-new novels every month. Bill me at the low price of $2.94 each plus 25¢ delivery and applicable sales tax, if any.* That's the complete price and a savings of over 10% off the cover prices—quite a bargain! I understand that accepting the books and gift places me under no obligation ever to buy any books. I can always return a shipment and cancel at any time. Even if I never buy another book from Harlequin, the 4 free books and the surprise gift are mine to keep forever.

181 BPA A3UQ

Name	(PLEASE PRINT)	
Address	Apt. No.	
City	State	Zip

This offer is limited to one order per household and not valid to present Harlequin Intrigue® subscribers. *Terms and prices are subject to change without notice. Sales tax applicable in N.Y.

UINT-696

©1990 Harlequin Enterprises Limited

DEBBIE MACOMBER

invites you to the

HEART OF TEXAS

Join Debbie Macomber as she brings you the lives
and loves of the folks in the ranching community
of Promise, Texas.

If you loved Midnight Sons—don't miss
Heart of Texas! A brand-new six-book series
from Debbie Macomber.

Available in February 1998
at your favorite retail store.

Heart of Texas by Debbie Macomber

Lonesome Cowboy	February '98
Texas Two-Step	March '98
Caroline's Child	April '98
Dr. Texas	May '98
Nell's Cowboy	June '98
Lone Star Baby	July '98

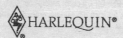
HARLEQUIN®

As Seen on TV!

Free Gift Offer

With a Free Gift proof-of-purchase
from any Harlequin® book, you can receive
a beautiful cubic zirconia pendant.

This stunning marquise-shaped stone is a genuine cubic
zirconia—accented by an 18" gold tone necklace.
(Approximate retail value $19.95)

Send for yours today...
compliments of ✦HARLEQUIN®

To receive your free gift, a cubic zirconia pendant, send us one original proof-of-purchase, photocopies not accepted, from the back of any Harlequin Romance®, Harlequin Presents®, Harlequin Temptation®, Harlequin Superromance®, Harlequin Love & Laughter®, Harlequin Intrigue®, Harlequin American Romance®, or Harlequin Historicals® title available at your favorite retail outlet, together with the Free Gift Certificate, plus a check or money order for $1.65 U.S./$2.15 CAN. (do not send cash) to cover postage and handling, payable to Harlequin Free Gift Offer. We will send you the specified gift. Allow 6 to 8 weeks for delivery. Offer good until March 31, 1998, or while quantities last. Offer valid in the U.S. and Canada only.

Free Gift Certificate

Name: _____

Address: _____

City: _____ State/Province: _____ Zip/Postal Code: _____

Mail this certificate, one proof-of-purchase and a check or money order for postage and handling to: HARLEQUIN FREE GIFT OFFER 1998. In the U.S.: 3010 Walden Avenue, P.O. Box 9071, Buffalo NY 14269-9057. In Canada: P.O. Box 604, Fort Erie, Ontario L2Z 5X3.

FREE GIFT OFFER   084-KEZ

ONE PROOF-OF-PURCHASE
To collect your fabulous FREE GIFT, a cubic zirconia pendant, you must include this
original proof-of-purchase for each gift with the properly completed Free Gift Certificate.

084-KEZR2